MW00755389

DOOMSDAY CLASSICS

SIGN OF THE LABRYS

Margaret St. Clair

Introduction by
Brian Stableford

DOVER PUBLICATIONS, INC.
Mineola, New York

Bibliographical Note

This Dover edition, first published in 2016, is a newly reset, unabridged republication of the work originally published by Bantam Books, New York, in 1963. An Introduction written by Brian Stableford has been specially prepared for the present edition.

Library of Congress Cataloging-in-Publication Data

Names: St. Clair, Margaret, author. | Stableford, Brian M., writer of introduction.
Title: Sign of the labrys / Margaret St. Clair ; introduction by Brian Stableford.
Description: Dover edition. | Mineola, New York : Dover Publications, 2016. |
 Series: Dover doomsday classics
Identifiers: LCCN 2016028876| ISBN 9780486804101 (softcover) | ISBN
 0486804100 (softcover)
Subjects: LCSH: Witches—Fiction. | Paranormal fiction. | BISAC: FICTION /
 Visionary & Metaphysical. | FICTION / Occult & Supernatural. | GSAFD:
 Science fiction. | Occult fiction. | Dystopias.
Classification: LCC PS3537.T112 S55 2016 | DDC 813/.54—dc23 LC record available at
https://lccn.loc.gov/2016028876

Manufactured in the United States
80410001   2016
www.doverpublications.com

Introduction by
BRIAN STABLEFORD

MARGARET ST. CLAIR's *Sign of the Labrys* was first published in 1963, when science fiction was in a period of economic transition. Having been confined to the pulp magazines for the first twenty-five years of its designation, it had been supplemented in the early 1950s by a number of magazines aiming at a higher level of literary sophistication, and also by the expansion of the paperback book market. Initially, science fiction paperbacks were almost entirely reprinted from the pulp magazines, but in the early 1960s a rapidly increasing quantity of fiction was written specifically for publication in that medium, taking advantage of a relative freedom from the confinement of the idiosyncratic expectations of a handful of magazine editors.

Margaret St. Clair had been a witness to and an active participant in those various transitions, adapting her work with considerable intelligence and artistry to the various opportunities they presented. She was perfectly content to write for the pulps, even though her style and interests were not well-adapted to the medium. St. Clair turned that very lack of adaptation into a strength, introducing an element of skeptical irony and subtle wit into her shorter works that made it appealing, even before she went to the unusual length of inventing a new alter ego, Idris Seabright, specifically in order to direct slicker and less programmatic short fiction at the most sophisticated of the new generation of fifties magazines, *The Magazine of Fantasy & Science Fiction*. She was a little less comfortable working at longer lengths. However, St. Clair's first novel, *Vulcan's Dolls*—unfortunately retitled *Agent of the Unknown* by its paperback publisher, an inveterate meddler with a tin ear—published in *Starling Stories* in 1952, is a bravura performance in what was known at the time as "vanVogtian" fiction, after its great pioneer, A. E. van Vogt.

Van Vogt was famous for the "intensive recomplication" of his plots and the frequent depiction of characters in the process of problematic and usually unwitting metamorphosis into superhumans. He also publicized his theory of genre writing, which involved careful adjustment of narrative pace to the pulp medium and the frequent use of "fictional sentences" specific to a genre. He thought that love stories, for instance, ought to contain as many sentences as possible with references to emotion, whereas science fiction stories ought to contain as many sentences as possible that left something deliberately unspecified or understated, hence creating a general ambience of enigmatic uncertainty.

Van Vogt's theory was widely mocked by people who could not understand it—although that did not stop some of them from attempting to use it—but Margaret St. Clair did understand it, and she put it into practice with a delicacy that van Vogt, who had a fondness for more garish melodrama, did not employ. The method is evident in all of her early novels, but *Sign of the Labrys* is the one where it reached its peak of achievement, and in which the particular ambience created by continual conscientious omission and understatement contrives a teasing perplexity that makes the novel highly distinctive and a fascinating delight to read. The title offers a perfect miniature of the strategy; the text eventually reveals, in passing, what a labrys is, but remains dutifully silent as to its signification.

Much of the commentary lavished on the novel since its first appearance (it has gained considerably in reputation over time) has been dedicated to filling in some of the background material that is left deliberately understated, observing that the author derived it from Gerald Gardner's *Witchcraft Today* (1954), a guidebook for lifestyle fantasy based on Margaret Murray's classic scholarly fantasy, *The Witch-Cult in Western Europe* (1921). Margaret and Eric St. Clair, her husband, subsequently adopted the "Wiccan" lifestyle fantasy in question, but that is of little relevance to the use made of the thesis for purely literary purposes in *Sign of the*

Labrys, where it is deftly used as an instrument of temptation and mystification.

Sign of the Labrys is a post-disaster story of a kind that had become commonplace in science fiction in the decade following the advent of the hydrogen bomb, which generated a great deal of unresolvable apocalyptic anxiety. The novel offers a striking image of post-holocaust society that is both appropriately alarming and intriguingly strange, to a surreal extent that is remarkable in itself, and the narrative uses that backdrop cleverly as a setting for a hectically fast-paced plot. The author's particular attitudes to the problems of fiction and life are developed on the one hand in the character of the hero, a far more modest and seemingly less omnicompetent individual than those featured in the macho science fiction typical of the era, and on the other in the hypothetical "solution" that the plot offers to the predicament of the stress-laden society depicted in the story.

Science fiction of the period had already developed the notion of comic breakout—salvation by spaceship—as standard solution to the problem of a spoiled Earth, to the extent that it had become something of a cliché. However, that did not fit in at all with Margaret St. Clair's worldview, and her plot only raises it briefly in order to reject it casually, determinedly setting its compass in another direction entirely. In doing so, it was not only original but somewhat ahead of its time, the value of the tired cliché having plunged dramatically once the Space Age was stillborn. It is not at all surprising that readers and critics who came across the book in later decades gradually realized that they had missed something interesting and valuable.

Some of them hastened to repair that omission by giving the author credit that had mostly passed her by while she was active, presumably somewhat to her regret, but authors have the privilege that their work can live on even when they are gone. It was the belated realization that *Sign of the Labrys* was a special book, deserving of a more appreciative audience, that made an eventual second edition necessary, and this one will be very welcome to connoisseurs of the genre.

1

THERE IS a fungus that grows on the walls that they eat. It is a violet color, a dark reddish violet, and tastes fresh and sweet. People go into the clefts to pick it.

The caves themselves are not very deep, though the excavated portions go much deeper. They were never actually occupied, and there had been no need for peace to be made for them to be abandoned entirely. People live in them now because they are quiet, even luxurious. There are stockpiles of everything in the world in the caves, if one only knows where to look. But of course there is not much smell of fresh air.

To get to where I live—in the tier called E3—you have to go through rooms filled with filing cabinets, computers, and refrigerators whose shelves hold tray after tray of spoiled anti-biotics. I know where I can get lots of flashlight bulbs, and the long detour doesn't bother me. I couldn't stand living on the surface, where the bulldozers keep one awake half the night with their clanking, and one is always likely to be forced into contact with people.

That night I had got home rather late. I don't know whether I have a job or not: I go there in the mornings, and sometimes they put me to work. Other times I stand around all day. The work is something any man with fair physical strength could do—moving boxes in a warehouse. I have moved the same stack of boxes over and over again. But it keeps one from thinking, and on Saturdays they give me a voucher. If they don't give me a voucher, it doesn't matter. I have a whole drawer full of them.

Anyhow, they had kept me late that night. When I got near my pad, I saw light coming out around the edges of the door. That meant there must be somebody inside. It bothered me.

It is odd how much we dislike contact with each other nowadays. Partly, of course, it is the habit of avoidance we all formed during the time the yeast plagues were so bad. But the plagues have been in abeyance for years now. B day—the time by which all the plague victims must be buried, to avoid new outbreaks—has been set forward a couple of times already, without anything happening. Still we stay away from each other. We want to be separate, apart. We can't stand each other's company.

And now there was somebody inside my pad. I didn't like it. I was in a bad mood when I went in.

He got up politely when I closed the door. He was a young, thin man in a dark plum-colored uniform. His hair and eyes were light.

"Mr. Sewell," he said, "I'm from the FBY. Here is my identification." He opened a little box and held it out to me.

I glanced inside. My heart was beating fast. As far as I could see, his identification was in order. "Umm," I said.

The FBY is not popular. It has no record of brutality, and, as far as we can be said to have a government nowadays, it is the FBY; I don't know why we dread it so. Perhaps it is the background of "science" which, to a man of my generation, is automatically dreadful. But there is a recurrent rumor that the organization is breeding yeasts for its own purposes. And the FBY men are a little too friendly, and at the same time a little too impersonal. The friendliness seems practiced, the impersonality contemptuous. As I said, they are not popular.

"Mr. Sewell," he said, smiling amiably, "I've come to you for information. My name, by the way is Ames, Clifford Ames. We've been told that you are in contact with a young woman whom we'd like very much to locate. Her name—at least, the name she is currently going under—is Despoina."

I raised my eyebrows. "I never heard the name before," I said. "It's an odd name."

"You don't have to answer me, of course," the FBY man answered, still smiling. "But it would be very much to your advantage to do so."

"My advantage?" I answered. "How can anything be to anyone's advantage nowadays?"

He laughed. "You have a point there," he conceded. "But we've been told that you're not only in contact with Despoina, or Spina, or just D, but that she's actually living with you."

"Living with me?" I was more surprised than annoyed. "Nobody's living with me. I couldn't stand it. If you searched my place, you wouldn't find any traces of feminine occupancy."

"None are evident, certainly. But we would very much like to locate her."

"I told you, I never heard the name before." His constant smiling was beginning to get on my nerves. "I don't know any young women, anyhow. Why are you hunting for this one? Wild yeasts?"

"We suspect she may be a sower."

A shiver ran down my spine. Sowers are people who, crazed by the destruction we've all lived through, deliberately disseminate neurolytic strains of yeasts. They are blind mass murderers. Or so it is said. Myself, I've never seen one.

"Even so, I can't help you," I said. "I just don't know anything."

"Our information—"

"You've been misinformed."

"I see." Ames moved toward the door. "You work long hours, don't you?" he said idly. "I waited for you a long time. Seven to six, you must work, or something like that."

"Seven to six!" It was my turn to laugh. "Oh, no, not even the bulldozer men, with B day to aim at, work hours like that. I don't even work eight to five."

Ames drew in his breath. I seemed to have said something significant without knowing it. He looked at me with kindling eyes. "Seven to six, eight to five, they add up to pretty much the same thing, don't they?" he said deliberately.

"By the way, I didn't give you a description of the girl we're hunting. She's said to be a little above medium height, slender and small-boned, with a remarkably fair skin. Unless she's cut it or dyed it, she has very heavy red-gold hair. Do you know anybody that looks like that?"

"I told you, I don't know any women at all. I haven't even spoken to a woman for two or three years, except to say good morning occasionally to the woman in the office where I work. And she's short and middle-aged."

"I see," he said again. "Well, if you change your mind and decide to cooperate with us, you can get in touch with me at this address." He handed me a card.

I took it, fuming. How neatly he'd given me the lie! "It's not a question of cooperation. I simply haven't anything to tell you. . . . Will you have any trouble finding your way back to the entrance? I can let you have an extra flashlight, if that would help." I wanted to get rid of him.

He opened the door of my pad and stepped out into the corridor. "Thank you, no. I know a shorter way."

While I looked on from the threshold, he unhooked a small tube from the array of gadgets that hung from his belt. He squinted up at the rough ceiling, as if hunting a particular spot. He moved the small tube so a beam from it would have described a circle on the ceiling, and after a second or two I felt a rush of cold air. There was a hole two feet across where the rough, dim ceiling of the corridor had been.

Ames hung the tube back on his belt and unhooked something else. It looked like a bunch of twine. He tossed this up into the hole. It spread out as it went up, and I saw it was an extremely light ladder of cord.

The FBY man put a hand on either side of it and began to climb. When he was halfway inside the hole, he called down something in a muffled voice that sounded like, "We FBY people can do magic too!"

He went on up. The cord ladder hung for a moment and then followed him. The dim ceiling became solid once more. The FBY man was gone.

I went back inside my pad. What I had just seen made me thoughtful. There was nothing inherently improbable in there being emergency exits at various spots in the caves, exits known only to a few. But what had Ames meant by his last remark? I was pretty sure I'd heard him correctly. Why had he said he could work magic *too?*

I shook my head. I started to the cupboard to get a can of stew for my supper, and then stopped. I really wasn't hungry. The interview with Ames had taken away my appetite, and in more senses than one. The conversation I'd had with him was the longest I'd had with anybody for years. So much human proximity was sickening. And on top of that, he was from the FBY.

In the end, I got out a bowl of the violet-colored fungus and supped on it. I had picked it only last week, and it was still sweet and fresh. It would have been better lightly boiled, but I was in no mood for cookery.

When I had eaten what I wanted, I put the bowl back. I tried to read—a textbook on bio-chemistry—but I couldn't keep my attention on the printed page.

At last I laid the book down. Despoina. A slender girl with red-gold hair and a very fair skin. Why did the FBY want her? And why did they think she was in contact with me?

2

IF WE human beings can bear each other's proximity for only a few minutes nowadays, it is odd how different the case is with the dead. On my way to work, I pass one of the vast fields where the plague victims lie, each in his yeast-proof plastic covering, awaiting burial. I feel no antipathy to *them*.

And yet, it could be horrible. The plastic coverings are translucent; one can catch glimpses of the puffy, unhappy dead within. But horror is absent. All I have ever felt is pity at the sight.

The bulldozers were working as I went by that morning. They are always working; there is even a night shift. The wonder is that they get so little done. I suppose the reason is partly the size of the task, and partly that not enough men, after all, are working at it. It is hard to find any inducement that is strong enough to make people work.

I got to the warehouse. The woman in the office nodded at me. The antipathy people feel toward each other nowadays is no less marked between males and females than it is between members of the same sex. People satisfy their sexual needs in fifteen-minute contacts, and run away from each other afterwards. It's not a way of living I care for. I don't suppose anybody likes it.

The foreman put me to work moving a stack of boxes. It was the same stack of boxes I had moved from the north side of the warehouse the day before yesterday. Now he was having me put them back there again.

As I worked, I thought about the man from the FBY. That organization (it was called into being when the plagues started, specifically to deal with the yeasts, but it was built upon an earlier organization) has always had the name of being closely knit. Are the FBY people somehow able to stand close contacts with each other, while the rest of us can't? Or is it merely their famous "discipline" that allows them to work together?

At noon, the foreman told me I could go home. As I left, I saw another of the warehouse workers moving my stack of boxes back to the south side.

The bulldozer men were eating lunch when I passed them. One of them, a small dark man, shouted at me, "Hey, Mac, how'd you like to run one of these things?"

I stopped. I yelled back, "You need men?"

"Sure. I'll teach you how to run this rig."

I spent the rest of the day learning how to operate a bulldozer, while the man who had called me "Mac" shouted instructions at me as often as needed.

By five I knew why the burials were going so slowly. In the first place, there weren't any diggers, and a bulldozer is an unsuitable rig with which to dig a burial ditch. And in the second place, there was no arrangement at all for moving the bodies into the trench. We had to scoop them up on the blades of the bulldozer and move them in, one at a time. But my feelings toward the bodies in their plastic bags did not change. They still filled me with pity, a sort of tenderness.

When I got home, I went to the sink to wash my hands. I turned on the tap. No water came out. This was serious.

All the rooms in E3—it was designed to house the more important government employees—contain a bunk, a sink, and a two-burner stove powered with batteries. There is a bath and a toilet for every four rooms. All the rooms in the tier draw water from a common reservoir.

I went into the room next to me, and turned on the water. No water came out. I hadn't thought it would.

Obviously, something was wrong with the reservoir. I didn't think the water supply was exhausted. It had been designed to last for half a century or so. What had probably happened was that a fungus growth had got into the main somewhere and stopped it up.

I'd have to move. Which way should it be, up or down?

The deeper one goes in the caves, the more luxurious the appointments get. But the thought of the deeper levels has always repelled me. . . . I'd try just a little lower, half a tier or so, and sideways.

I packed up what I wanted to take with me—a few books, a Go board, and an assortment of canned and dehydrated foods. I could always get more foods from the stockpiles, of course, but these were things I particularly liked. Then I started out.

A suitcase in either hand, I walked along the dim corridor until I came to F1 (this is a tier, and different from F, which is a separate level). Then I walked down a couple of steps and turned left.

I had not gone far along the Fl tier before I saw that one of the red lights in a signal panel on the corridor wall was blinking. That meant something had gone wrong along the tier; what, I couldn't guess. It probably wasn't serious, or the whole system would have been shut off, except for emergency exits.

I hesitated. Should I turn back? But F2 was a little deeper than I liked, and besides, I was curious. I walked on.

A door opened as I drew abreast of it. A man appeared in the opening, holding onto the door frame. He was staggering on his feet. I thought he must be sick or drunk.

He made a noise in his throat, and then the word "seven" came out. He gasped desperately, struggled for breath, and collapsed at my feet.

I had an instant of panic. I had seen people die like that before, when the plagues were so bad. But of course this man might just be drunk. From a little distance, I examined him,

Now, there are—were—two main types of yeast plague. The commoner was the pulmonary, in which the yeast cells proliferated within the lungs to the extent that the victim could no longer breathe, and died, essentially, of asphyxiation. The bodies of people who died of this form were characteristically bloated and puffed. The other form was the neurolytic. The yeast cells secreted an enzyme that destroyed the conductivity of nerve cells, and death followed so quickly after the ingestion of the yeasts that the victim seemed to have been struck by an invisible lightning flash. He died before he knew anything was happening to him.

The man on the corridor floor near my feet was wearing the dark plum-colored uniform of the FBY. Even as I watched, the seams of his neat, braid-trimmed tunic snapped under the pressure of the swelling flesh inside. His bloated chest showed through the gaps. There was no doubt that he was dead. And there was no doubt that what had killed him was the pulmonary form of the yeast plague.

The yeast cells are air-borne and easily disseminated. With my suitcases still in my hand, I turned and ran back the way I had come.

I stopped when I was back in E3 again. I was really frightened. Pulmonary plague takes about two hours to kill, after exposure, and I certainly had been exposed. I spent the next two hours sitting on the bed in my old pad, listening to myself breathe, and coughing and inhaling experimentally.

Seven o'clock came, and I was still alive. Either none of the yeast cells had reached me, or I had a natural immunity.

I drew a deep breath. I still had to think about getting another place to live, and I hadn't had any supper. And what ought I to do about the dead man on the F1 tier? The disposal people ought to be told, so he could be sprayed and put in one of the plastic bags for burial. But I hated to get mixed up in it.

In the end, I decided it was the FBY's problem. They were said to keep in close touch with their people; they were sure to find this one soon.

This time I went the other way in the corridor, toward level D. The accommodations on this level—half-level, actually—are for three or four people, and not at all on the plushy side. I settled at last on a room with no furniture except four rather Spartan bunks. But the lights and water worked, and there was the same old two-burner electric plate. Now, what about something to eat?

I looked over my store of food. I was hungry, but nothing sounded good. What I really wanted, of course, was some of the violet-colored fungus.

People eat the fungus because it is almost the only fresh, unprocessed foodstuff that we have. When the yeast cells escaped from the scientists who had been working with them, and started the great plagues, it was not only the sorts that were deleterious to human beings that escaped. Our domestic animals died too—the mortality was even higher among them—and our food plants too were affected.

Some food plants became extinct—wheat, for example, and barley and rice. Woody plants of all sorts died. I haven't seen a tree for nearly ten years. And the germ cells of the common vegetables, like lettuce and tomatoes, mutated to become polyploid. Nowadays a lettuce plant is ten feet tall, covered with a sort of bark, and about as edible as a floor mop.

But the fungus is good, fresh and crisp and sweet. When it is lightly boiled, it tastes a lot like water chestnuts. And one never gets tired of its taste. The only trouble is finding it. It grows beyond the part of the caves that has been furnished for people, on the bare face of the rock.

I took a melmac tray and a knife from one suitcase. If one cuts the fungus fronds with a knife, rather than just tearing them loose, they grow back again. I stuck a flashlight in my belt, and started out.

The place I was going was at the end of E3, my old tier. The fungus probably grew a lot of other places too, but I was sure of that one.

It was a longish, rather tiring walk. There was considerable clambering about needed for me to reach the sloping cleft where the fungus grew. I had to go on hands and knees for the last few feet. But the fungus had grown back luxuriantly since my last visit, and I filled my tray easily.

I started to back out of the cleft. My belt caught on a projection on the rock, and the flashlight stuck in it jerked up. I saw, rudely scratched on the rough rock, an outsized figure seven.

My heart jumped. I took the flashlight from my belt and examined the sign carefully. No, it wasn't a seven, but a much older symbol. Somebody—it must have been quite difficult to do—had drawn on the grayish stone the old, old sign of the labrys, the double-headed axe.

I thought about it most of the way back to my new pad. The sign might have been there before, but I didn't think so; when I had first gone fungus-hunting, I'd searched that particular cleft thoroughly. But if somebody had only recently scratched it, who? And why? As far as I knew, I was the only person who even knew of the existence of the cleft. For a moment of mental vertigo, I wondered whether I myself could possibly have drawn the sign on the rock. But I knew that I had not.

Back at my new lodging, I washed the fronds of fungus and put them on to cook with a cube of dehydrated beef broth. But I was fated to have trouble with supper that night. When I went to my other suit-case for a food bowl, I found an oblong of paper resting on top of it.

It was a note. The note, written in pale brown ink, was quite short: "Mr. Sewell, come to the lower gallery at about eleven tonight." It was signed with a "D".

I started to crumple the paper up angrily. Ames, the FBY man, must have left it, and it must represent either an attempt to embroil me actively with the mysterious Despoina, or, more likely, a trial at forcing guilty knowledge from me.

Then I stopped. How had Ames known where to find me? I hadn't known, myself, that I was going to select a pad on level D until the last moment. For him to be able to find me ten minutes after I moved in must mean that the FBY was keeping me under constant surveil-lance. And if they were watching me that closely, they ought to know that I wasn't in contact with Despoina, and never had been.

I picked up the note and examined it more closely. The ink it was written in was so thick it seemed embossed on the paper, a pale brown paste that might almost have been put on with a brush. The handwriting itself was large, bold, and elegant. It was surprisingly easy to read. A woman's writing? Yes, if she was rather egoistical.

I ate my supper. I felt restless. I wasn't going to go, of course. But at fifteen minutes to eleven, quite as if I had meant to go all along, I loaded fresh batteries into my flashlight and left my pad.

The lower gallery is in its natural state. When the caves were fit-ted out for human habitation and the lower levels were dug, it was considered too weak structurally to be used. It remains exactly what it always was—a huge room, two hundred by three hundred feet, with a low roof and a few stalactites. It isn't even spectacular. I met nobody on the way. There must be a good many other people living in the caves, but we almost never encounter each other. When we do, we look aside. It's better that way.

The gallery, of course, was completely dark. I shone the little beam of my flashlight as far as it would reach, and made a partial circuit of the walls. . . . Nobody. But the place was so big a dozen people could have been lurking out of reach of my beam.

I waited. I kept the light on and the beam moving about in the darkness. At last I heard a noise. It sounded like a step. I called, "Who's there?"

There was no answer. I was getting fed up, and turned to go back.

A breath of air blew past me. It was cool and moist-smelling. And then a voice, toneless and echoless, spoke, it seemed into my very ear: "Blessed . . . be . . ."

I wheeled around. I sent the beam of light stabbing out into the darkness. "Who's there?" I called. "Where are you? Come out! Come out!"

My shouts died away. There was no answer, nothing. Not even a footfall. Nothing at all.

3

I SLEPT late next morning, a cold, unrefreshing sleep, and got to my new job late. It didn't matter. I worked the rest of the day with the bulldozer. It was odd how peaceful I felt doing it.

When I got back to my new pad at the end of the day, Ames was waiting for me.

"How did you know where to find me?" I asked.

He shrugged. "When I found you'd moved, it was just a question of guessing to which level you'd go, and of opening doors."

"Umm. What do you want?"

"What I wanted last time. For you to put me in contact with Despoina."

"I told you, I don't have any contact with her."

"Oh? Then how do you account for this?" He held out the note that had come last night. Like a fool, I had forgotten to destroy it.

"The note was left without any action on my part. I don't know why it was left."

"Did you keep the rendezvous?" he asked eagerly.

". . . Yes."

"What happened?"

"Nothing."

"Nothing at all? I can't believe that."

"I thought I heard a footstep," I answered unwillingly. "And then a voice said, 'Blessed be.' I don't know who or where the speaker was."

His face had begun to glow. "'Blessed be'!" he repeated softly. "Yes, it's certainly she." And then, to me, "Take me to her, Sewell."

"If I could—I can't—but if I could, why do you want her?"

"My organization—No harm will come to her."

I laughed. "You don't sound as if it was an organizational matter. You seem to be personally involved."

"No . . ." he said, and then seemed to reconsider. "I've been infected with the plague," he said slowly. "She can cure such things."

I backed away from him. "Which form?"

"A new form. I'll be dead in a couple of weeks."

"You've got a hell of a nerve coming here."

"You're in no danger, Mr. Sewell. You don't seem to be aware of it, but I can assure you it's true: you're plague-immune."

I eyed him appraisingly. He didn't look sick; he looked elated. "How could she help you? You said the first time she was a sower of plague."

"Did I say that? She can kill plague cells just by looking at them."

This wasn't absolutely impossible. I had heard stories of such things when the plagues were at their height. But somehow, I didn't believe him. My mind put him down as a rotten liar, for all his clean-cut face and his braid-trimmed uniform.

"It isn't good enough," I said finally. "If I could take you to her—I can't—but if I could," I said again, "I'd have to have a better reason than that."

His face cracked. It was like a piece of paper being crumpled, or an ice floe breaking up. "I've got to have her!" he cried desperately. "How long can I go on living like this?"

"Like what?" I asked.

"Perhaps you're so numb you don't suffer," he answered. "Perhaps you're so numb that you don't realize you're suffering. But I was—close to her, two or three years ago. When the ice thaws a little, you realize how much our isolation from each other hurts us."

"That's how everybody lives nowadays," I replied. "We can't stand each other's company."

"Yes. But it used to be different. People could share things, work together, build and create. Everything rested on that. The ties between human beings were the basis of all societies. Now those ties have failed. And we don't feel or think like human beings any more."

I was getting uneasy. It wasn't only what he was saying; it was his mere physical presence. I wanted him to go. I said, "These are philosophical questions, Mr. Ames. Let's keep it on a personal level. Were you in love with this girl?" The words sounded strange as they left my mouth.

"I don't know," he said. He was trembling, a slight tremor that came in recurrent waves. "It doesn't matter. She—don't you understand, you fool?—she could take away the numbness.

"You're younger than I am," he went on. "Perhaps that's what makes you a fool. You haven't lived long enough to learn that there's horror underneath the ice."

I sighed. "I still can't take you to her. Since it's a personal matter, and not an institutional interest of the FBY, perhaps you won't mind telling me what makes you think I can."

"You're one of the same kind."

"What do you mean by that?" I said. (I was almost at the end of my tether: in a minute or two I was going to try to throw him out bodily. We weighed about the same, but he was an inch or two taller. And he probably had had more training in hand-to-hand combat than I.) "Do you think I can give you a feeling of being 'close,' somehow thaw out the ice?"

"You're one of the same kind as she is, but you don't know it," he replied evasively. "You have all the signs."

"What signs?"

He didn't answer. I advanced a step or two toward him. He drew back a little, as if he felt the almost instinctive dislike of contact with another person that we all have.

"What signs?" I repeated. "What kind of person is Despoina, if I'm like her?"

He had stopped trembling. He smiled at me quite cheerfully. "I'll tell you," he said, "because it won't make any sense to you. By the time you do realize what I mean, it will be too late.

"You're the same kind of person as Despoina. Despoina is a witch."

4

A WITCH is an old woman who rides through the air on a broom-stick. . . . I was lying on my bunk, thinking, after Ames had left. If one took this definition literally, Ames's remark was obvious non-sense. He had said Despoina was young, he had implied that she was beautiful (slender figure, very fair skin, heavy red-gold hair). And nobody, young or old, can fly through the air on a broomstick.

A witch is a woman who has made a compact with the devil so she can harm her neighbors' cattle and crops. But the only devil I have ever encountered has been my fellow human beings, and nobody has cattle or crops to be damaged nowadays.

I sighed and punched up the bunk's pillow. What had Ames meant, anyway? And he had said I was like her, I was one of the same sort.

Lying on my back, with my arms under my head, I reviewed my past. I had been born in Peabody, a smallish town in Massachusetts, twenty-five years ago. Mother had been a kind and sensible woman; my childhood had been a happy one. The thing I remembered most vividly about those years was her wonderful baking: the slabs of salt-rising bread, malodorous but delicious, and thickly buttered; the cookies; the pies; the delicate rolls.

When I was fifteen, the plagues had come. Only a few cases at first, baffling to the doctors; and then a flood, an overwhelming torrent, of deaths.

I had survived. It occurred to me now that perhaps I owed my survival to my mother's fondness for baking, to all the wild yeasts, baked into harmlessness, I had chewed and swallowed in the form of salt-rising bread. Ames had said I was immune, and perhaps I was; this was as good a way as any other to account for it.

The plagues had been really virulent for five years, five years of increasing social disorganization and failure of contact. I had seen a lot of people die. And then, for me, five years of drifting, of aimless and indifferent wandering.

That brought me up to the present. I couldn't see that anything in it made me a witch.

I got up from the bunk and made myself some supper. The simplest way of accounting for Ames's various statements was to assume that he was self-deluded; he had made all of it, or most of it, up. The only evidence of Despoina's existence I had had so far could have originated with him. There is nothing in the rules that says an FBY man can't be a little mad.

I ate, read for a while, and crawled in between the bunk's paper sheets. I woke about two o'clock in the morning, from an indifferent dream, to a sensation of abysmal horror and hopelessness.

It was so bad that I sat up in the darkness, shaking. At last I roused myself to turn on the light, but that didn't help. Ames had said that there was horror under the ice; it seemed that the ice had melted a little and let some of the horror through. What bothered me as much as anything was the awareness that I could die where I lay and my body not be found for weeks—if, indeed it was ever found. There was a peculiarly blank quality to my fear, a horror of emptiness.

At last the emotion subsided a little. I went to one of my suitcases and got out a book on set theory. I forced myself to keep my attention on the printed page.

At first I'd have fits of shaking, when I'd stop reading and be locked in a glassy fixation on my own isolatedness. But little by little I grew interested in what the book was saying; finally, after a couple of hours, I got sleepy. I left the light on and, with the book on my chest, went back to sleep.

I showed up at the bulldozers at the usual time next morning. The day went calmly enough until mid-afternoon. Then, as I lifted one of the big plastic-covered parcels on the blade of the bulldozer, I saw that the body inside it was moving torpidly.

It was a man; I could make him out well enough to see the buttons on his coat. His body was still, but his arms and legs moved up and down slowly, as if he were languidly trying to swim.

I gave a cry. I dropped the bundle back on the ground and jumped down from the seat of the bulldozer. I ran over to Jim, the small dark man who was responsible for my being on the dozer crew.

"One of the bodies—it's alive," I said.

"You think so?" He laughed. He walked over to the bulldozer with me and looked at the man.

"Naw," he said. "He's dead for sure. They do that sometimes. It's the gas. You just haven't happened to see one before." He walked away.

I got back on the seat of the bulldozer. I went on with my job. But I did not disturb the man who had been moving. I buried other people for the rest of the day.

When I got back to my pad, I was tired. I had a shower—the water was only lukewarm on this level—and then went to my suitcase for fresh paper clothes. As I raised the lid, something slid off and fell ringingly on the floor.

What had it been? I bent over and looked for it. At last, under the bunks on the far side, I located it. It was a gold ring.

It was set with a flat elliptical stone, carnelian I thought, engraved in intaglio. I took it under the light by my bunk to see what the subject was.

It was a woman, naked to the waist, with her hair in long ringlets. Her hands were under her breasts, supporting them, and she wore a flounced skirt that reached to her feet. Her feet seemed to be tied together—but *it* was difficult to be certain about this detail—with a cord.

Altogether, an odd gem. The woman's costume looked Cretan. It was hard to believe I held in my hand anything that had come down through so many centuries, but the gold of the hoop and bezel seemed pitted and old.

I tried it on. The hoop was too small for any of my fingers except the little one, and even there it had to be worked carefully over the joint. I took the ring off again and was still looking at it when there came a rap at my door.

"Come in," I said.

It was Ames. His eyes were wild; he looked as if he hadn't slept. "I came to ask—What's that in your hand?"

I closed my fingers over the ring. "Nothing," I said.

"Oh, yes it is." A stun pistol was suddenly in his hand. "Give it to me," he ordered.

I hesitated. But the ring had come to me unsought, and there was really no reason why he couldn't look at it if he wished. Silently I handed it to him.

He drew in his breath. "It's Despoina's ring," he said. "I've seen it on her hand a thousand times. How did you *get* it?"

"It was lying on the lid of my suitcase when I got home."

"And no message? But I know what it means. She's sent it to you as a passport, so you can get past the guards. She wants you to go to her."

"Past what guards? Where? And if she wants me to go to her, why doesn't she just tell me so?"

"The guards on the lower levels," he said, as if to a child. "I ought to have realized where she was when she told you to meet her in the lower gallery. But you couldn't get through, of course, without something to get past the guards."

I looked at him. He was turning the ring over and over in his fingers, with his mouth open. "Mr. Ames," I said, "I don't believe a word of this. Is there any such person as Despoina? For all I know, you left the ring on my suitcase yourself."

He laughed. "I could have, couldn't I?" There was a crafty gleam in his eyes. He was still fondling the ring.

I hesitated. It was reasonable to assume that if I told him he could have the ring, that he had my permission to go in my stead on a visit to the mythical Despoina with the ring as his passport, he would go away with it, happy and satisfied, and leave me in peace. He was unbalanced, certainly, but I did not really think he had left the ring himself.

"I—" I began, and stopped. I remembered the horror of empti-ness that had come on me last night. "Give me my ring," I said.

He looked at me. Deliberately he slipped the ring on over his little finger; his hands were smaller than mine. "It's mine now," he told me. His stun pistol was covering me.

"Oh, hell. Keep it, then, if you want it so much." I managed a shrug. Then I jumped for his throat.

The stun pistol went off. I felt the tingling paralysis run along my right arm. But I still had the use of my left hand, and I had taken him off guard. In a moment we were rolling on the floor.

He was a dirty fighter, and he knew about pressure points. And I had only one arm. For a minute or two I managed to hold my own and even cut off his wind temporarily. Then he got uppermost and started to bang my head against the floor.

Abruptly I felt his body relax. I went for his throat again; I thought it might be a trick. But he felt limp and heavy. When he didn't move, I pushed him off me and got to my feet.

His face was flushed and his mouth was open. I felt for his pulse, and couldn't find any. A trickle of greenish slime ran from his mouth.

For a moment I didn't understand. Then I realized what it was. He was dead. It was the neurolytic form of the plague.

How had it reached him? And why hadn't it reached me? I sank down on my bunk, panting. After a moment I shook my head. I didn't know the answer to any of it.

I got up and went over to Ames's body. I pulled the ring off his finger and carefully put it on my own.

He had said Despoina had sent the ring as a passport. He had said she wanted me to go to her. Very well. Despoina might or might not have any real existence. But I would go.

5

THE LIGHT brightens as you descend in the levels until, abruptly, you reach the dark. Or at least that is the story. I mean by this that there was no reason why I should wait for day to go in search of Despoina, or think that night would be any advantage to me. But I was tired and hungry, and I couldn't decide what to do about Ames.

I stood looking at him. The trickle of slime had reached his chin and was trailing down on the collar of his uniform. He had called on me in a private capacity, which meant that the FBY probably wasn't keeping track of him. If I went off and left him lying there, his body would decay slowly for several weeks, during all of which time, spores of the neurolytic form of the plague would be getting into the ventilating system. And, of course, anyone who opened the door of the room where he was would be dead in a few seconds; I'd be leaving a nasty, deadly little booby trap behind.

On the other hand, Ames had died during a struggle with me, in a room where I was currently living. If I reported him to the disposal people, there might be trouble with the FBY. And I wanted to be on my way as soon as I rested and ate.

This inability to decide what to do, this nagging irresolution, and in a matter where I would ordinarily have been decisive enough, was the first sign of a bodily change in me. But I did not recognize it for what it was.

At last I decided to go up to B level, taking my personal belongings with me, and put in an anonymous call for the disposal people. Even then, I could not bring myself to leave at once. I stood over

Ames irresolutely, wondering whether to take his belt, with its collection of weapons and gadgets—it might be useful—but fearing vaguely that it might be evidence against me. Even after I had got to the door with my suitcases, I turned back to stand over him for several minutes more. Finally, I almost ran out of the room. I didn't take the belt.

I left my bags in a community kitchen on C, went up to B, and made my anonymous call. In the kitchen—there was nobody else there, of course—I made some soup from concentrate and opened a can of meat balls. The food didn't taste good, and I left most of it. And now, where should I sleep?

I thought of the rows and rows of rooms and smaller cubicles, the accommodations for a city, almost a people, of troglodytes. On any individual level each bed was exactly like any other bed.

Sweat began to run down my body; my hands were trembling. I was in a state of acute, unreasonable bodily panic. I licked my lips. Very well then, I'd sleep—I'd sleep—

It seemed to me that the only possible place for rest for me tonight was in the cleft at the end of E3, where I had seen the sign of the labrys scratched upon the bare stone.

Again, this whim, this fancy, didn't alarm me. I went into one of the dorms, stripped the foam mattress off a bunk, roiled it up. It made a carryable parcel. After more indecision, I left my suitcases in the kitchen and, with my mattress, went back to E3.

It took me quite a long time to maneuver and push my mattress into the spot where I wanted it. I kept breaking into drenching sweats and stopping to rest.

At last I got it laid out in a reasonably smooth and level space on the stone. The sign of the double axe was above and to the left of my bed, and clumps of the purple fungus were growing behind it. There was a faint draft of air through the cleft, and I could see, though a long way off, the dim glow of the illuminated corridors of E3. I lay down facing it. It did not occur to me to wonder why I had gone to so much trouble to spend a comfortless night lying on the rock. Before I went to sleep I held Despoina's ring up before my eyes. But the light was too poor for me to make out anything except the ellipsoidal shape of the stone.

I slept surprisingly well. Once I half roused up, with the impression that people were going past, a long way off, in the dim corridors of E3. I thought sleepily that they must be the disposal people, come to get Ames's body, but this was almost certainly wrong; he was in level D, the one above this one, and there would be no reason for them to go this deep.

I woke after seven and a half hours. I sat up on my mattress and yawned and stretched. My muscles were a little sore, and my skin was warm. As I crawled out of the cleft, I felt a transient dizziness.

Outside, in E3 once more, I took stock of myself. I wasn't hungry, and there was no point in taking food into the lower levels, which were said to be better stocked than the upper ones were. In my pockets and on my belt I had a flashlight, a water flask, and a pocketknife. That was all. I might not need any of them. Perhaps it would have been wise to have taken Ames's stun pistol, but it was too late now. I doubted that weapons would help me much anyway. I would have to trust to luck primarily—and to Despoina's ring.

The water in my flask was down, and I tried to fill it at a fountain before I remembered that something was wrong with the water supply on tier E3. Well, I'd fill it in F. I wanted to get started. I walked toward the stairs.

It is important to understand what a level is. It is not much like a floor in an office building. A level may be a hundred or a hundred and fifty feet deep, and subdivided into several tiers. Also, access to them is not uniform. The upper levels are simple and straightforward; one gets to and from them by stairs, escalators, or elevators. I dislike the elevators, myself, since if the power should be interrupted, one would be stuck there indefinitely. But the upper levels are easy.

As one goes down, it gets difficult. Entrances and exits are usually concealed. The reason for this, I think, was partly to protect the VIP's in the lower levels from unauthorized intrusion, partly to provide a redoubt in case the "enemy" was victorious, and partly because of the passion for secrecy that characterizes the military mind.

Whatever the reason, the difficulty exists. F is said to be the last of the levels one can enter easily,

I started down the stairs. They were steep and tedious. I knew there must be an escalator somewhere, but I didn't want to spend time hunting for it.

The stairs turned a couple of times and then stopped on a landing. I was sure this wasn't F, but one of the sublevels, and I poked around, opening doors and going down short corridors, until I found a descending staircase again. It was so steep I was sure it was a maintenance flight, but it would get me there just the same.

The stairway stopped several times, but I always managed to find where it went on again. At last I stood on level F.

I don't know what I had been expecting. Ames had spoken of guards, but it wasn't reasonable to think they'd be posted as far up as level F.

F had been designed as the laboratory level, but there had been a foul-up during its construction. Fl and F2, the partial levels, or tiers, which had been meant to house the lab workers of F, had been constructed above it and on the bias, like the two arms of a Y. The partial levels were a considerable distance from the primary they were supposed to serve, and I don't know what would have happened if the levels had ever been inhabited as intended; I suppose the lab workers would have commuted to work.

The part of F where I now was seemed to be a service area: there were doors marked "High Voltage" and "Maintenance," and the corridor was narrow and high. It ran straight for six or eight feet, and then seemed to descend a couple of steps.

There was a drinking fountain on my left, and I filled my flask at it. The water ran fresh enough, but it had a sulphury smell. I found it faintly nauseating.

I stoppered the flask, put it back on my belt, and walked along the corridor to where it changed level. There I stopped in surprise.

The space in front of me was large, perhaps twenty by fifty feet, and it was carpeted with a dense deep covering of shining white. The covering was hummocky and uneven, though always seeming to be thick, and I stared at it, wondering what the fabric was. Fabric? Or was it a fungus? Then I saw that the hummocks were constantly moving, and my heart gave a jump.

The space before me, from wall to wall, was filled with white rats.

They moved and humped and opened their mouths at each other; they were packed in as tight as sardines in a can; no wonder I had thought them a particularly dense rug.

Two stair treads, some nine inches high, separated me from them. Unhurriedly I descended the steps and stepped out on the rats. I tried to push them away with my toes before I put my feet down; I disliked the idea of feeling them crunching under my feet.

The result of my first three paces was astonishing. I had tried to avoid stepping on the rats, but I had felt one of them give under me. Now, all about my feet and widening out from them, the rats began to die. They gasped and writhed, turned on their backs, collapsed in ever-broadening circles about me. It was like watching the ripples spread out from a rock thrown in a pool.

The ripples of death seemed to die away and turn inward. The rats on the periphery were coming toward the center. Watching in fascinated disgust, I saw that they were coming toward me, feeding ravenously on the ones that were dead.

The eaters wavered. For a moment they were immobile, their snouts raised. Then, as if they had heard a signal, inaudible to me, they turned and scurried away, some of them toward the end of the open space, others through a series of low openings along the wall.

It was like watching water running down the drain in a sink. I think it cannot have been more than sixty seconds until the whole space in front of me was empty, leaving only three clusters of dead rats.

I drew an astonished breath. After a moment I began to walk forward, avoiding the clumps of rats. My body was bathed in warm sweat.

Far down the corridor from me a door opened and a girl stepped out.

She was wearing a white lab smock and a checked wool skirt; even in the high-heeled slippers she had on, she was short. Her dark short hair curled loosely about her ears. Her skin had a pale, pearly luster, oddly pale for the rest of her coloring and her dark red lips. In one hand she had some sort of hilted knife. I did not realize until much later that it was an athame.

Her eyes widened when she saw me. She hesitated and then started toward me, her hands at her side.

"What happened to the rats?" I asked when she was still some distance off. I hadn't meant to say that.

'They went back to their cages," she replied absently. "Eight to five."

"Ten to three," I answered automatically. "Don't come any closer to me."

"Why not?" she asked. But she slowed down and looked at me.

"I'm a vector of neurolytic plague."

She laughed. It was not a response I would have expected anybody to make to what I had said.

"What makes you think that?" she asked.

"The rats. They died as soon as I got near them. It must have been plague."

She laughed again. Her laugh, like her voice, was husky and low. "Well, it wasn't," she answered. "They died because there's a constitutional imbalance in their brains, and any unexpected jar kills them. It's related to their four-hour tropism out of their cages and back again.

"Who are you, anyway?" she went on. "You gave me the password, but I don't think you're Gerald. You don't look like the description of him at all."

"Gerald is dead," I answered confidently.

"How do you know?"

"I saw him die. It was on F1 a couple of days ago. He died of the pulmonary form of the plague." As I spoke, I had a vivid picture of the FBY man's bloated body lying at my feet. It did not occur to me to wonder why I was so confident he was the "Gerald" she was speaking of.

"Oh." She tossed the hilted knife up in the air and caught it again by the handle—expertly, like a juggler. "So she was wrong, then," she said thoughtfully.

"So who was wrong?" I asked.

"Don't you know?" she countered. "And you haven't told me yet who you are."

I felt a surge of half-grudging attraction to the girl. I supposed that in a few moments I would begin to want to get away from her; but for the present I felt oddly contented in her company. Besides, there was really no reason why I shouldn't answer her. "My name's Sam Sewell," I said. "I'm trying to find the exit from level F to the one below."

She was silent for a long minute. Then she said, "Go ahead. I wish you luck."

"Do you know where the exits are?"

"One of them. There are several. But I only know one."

She had turned and was walking slowly along beside me down the open space. There were faint clankings from behind us, and I turned around to see a two-foot-tall robot, not at all humanoid, sweeping the dead white rats into a sort of dustpan.

"Does it always do that?" I asked her.

"Yes. Otherwise this level would soon be uninhabitable."

A door ahead of us on the left opened, and a fattish man in shirt sleeves stepped out. When he saw us he darted back inside.

"Who was that?" I asked her.

"I don't know. A man."

"You're not the only one living on this level?"

"No, of course not. There are two or three hundred labs down here, some of them very well equipped. When the plagues came, not all of the scientific workers died. Some of them came down here so they could go on with their work, and some of them just came down here anyway."

"Since you know where one of the exits is, won't you show it to me?"

She gave a very slight shrug. "Come along to my office. We can talk it over."

We had reached the door from which she had originally come. I started to turn into it, but she pulled me on.

"That's not my office. I just happened to come out of there."

"Do you eat and sleep down here?" I asked.

"Uh-huh. I brought a mattress and cooking stuff down from F2. I'm comfortable enough. I take baths in a big laboratory sink."

The wide space ended and a narrow corridor turned left. The light was different here—a little dimmer, and with a faint orange cast.

We had gone about fifteen feet in the new direction when she pressed down on my shoulders. "Bend over," she said "It's dangerous."

"Dangerous? Why?"

"Don't you know? Can't you tell?"

"No, not at all."

She sighed. "The lab animals always get out of the way of ionizing radiation, if they have a chance. I'd think you'd be sensitive to this."

"Well, I'm not. What is it?"

"Somebody in the lab up ahead has hauled a big X-ray machine up close to the wall. He's got all the voltage going into it that it will take. The beam is going across the corridor at about the height of a man's heart. It might not kill you for a while. But there are an awful lot of roentgens there."

"But why? Why would anybody do that?"

"I don't know. He may have something in a cage on the other side of the corridor that he wants to irradiate, something that can't be moved. Or he may be trying to put up some sort of barrier against movement in the corridor. I don't know what his motive is. But it's dangerous. Bend down."

We had stopped walking while we talked. Now, crouched over so that we were not more than three feet above the floor, we moved forward again.

"You can straighten up now," she said presently.

I stood up. My body felt shaky, and sweat was once more running down my sides.

"Are there any more booby traps like that?" I asked.

"I don't think so. We're almost there. . . . Don't you feel well?"

I considered. "I'm a little light-headed."

"Ah." She opened a door on the right. "This is my office."

I followed her inside. She motioned me to a chair and sat down herself, across a desk from me.

It was oddly like a doctor's office—the straight wooden chairs, the desk, and she herself, careful, attentive, and with the impersonal attractiveness a good woman physician has. But the knife lay between us on the blotter of the desk. I could not take my eyes from it.

"Now," she said, "you want me to show you the exit from F to the level below."

"Yes. That's the idea."

"Why do you want to go on down?"

"I've been sent for."

"Ah. But why should I show you the way?"

I hesitated. Then I held out my hand toward her so she could see Despoina's ring.

Her eyes flickered. She stretched out one hand and touched the bezel of the ring lightly. "Yes . . . I will help you." Before I could feel elated, she added, "But you must give me the ring."

"How can I do that?" I asked. "It's my passport through G. I'd never get any deeper without it."

She shrugged. There was a scurrying noise. It sounded like leaves falling, like rain, like big particles of mist blowing against a window. I said, "What's that?"

"The rats. They come out every four hours."

"But—it hasn't been four hours since I first got to F."

"Oh, yes it has. Doesn't it seem that long to you?"

"No, not at all."

"That's odd." She looked at me quickly and then looked away again. "It sounds as if you were one of the old—"

"Old what?"

"You'll find out later. Well, then, I'll help you, and you needn't give me the ring. But you must make me a promise first. I'll tell you what it is as you go through. Long enough before you go through for you to stop if you like. . . . Come into the next room."

The adjoining room was also like a doctor's office. There was a flat couch, an enameled table with rubber gloves and jars of solutions on it, and an outsized autoclave. But in one corner there was a chair with arms and straps along the arms. I looked down and saw that there were straps at the legs of the chair too.

"Sit down there," she said. She was unsmiling. "There are things I must do before I can help you through."

I looked at the chair. Straps and . . . "Suppose I refuse?" I asked.

"Then you can hunt the exit yourself." She laughed. "You'll never find it. Or any of the others, as far as that goes."

"But what are you going to do to me?"

"If I told you ahead of time," she said, "it wouldn't work." She hesitated. "There isn't anything else I *can* do," she said at last. "Sit down."

The atmosphere impressed me as sinister, and yet I felt confidence in her. I seated myself on the hard leather pad of the chair, and she stooped and buckled the straps around my legs.

"Now your arms." She fastened the straps there too.

"I feel pretty helpless," I said, trying to speak as if it were a joke.

"You have to be," she answered.

I was buckled down. She went over to the enameled table and busied herself with something. At last she turned around.

What she was holding in her hands surprised me. I don't know exactly what I had been expecting—a hypodermic needle, perhaps, or a surgical knife. But what she had was something that would have been at home on a woman's dressing table—an ordinary looking glass. The frame and handle were of chased silver.

She walked over to me and held it in front of my face. "What do you see?" she asked.

"My own face."

"How does it look?"

"Lopsided." This was true. "And I'm sweating more than I thought I was."

"Umm." She put the glass down. She chewed her lip for a moment. Then she got an ampoule from a cabinet in the corner. She broke it under my nose.

"Breathe in deep," she said tonelessly. "Hold it in your lungs."

I obeyed. The substance in the ampoule was aromatic, like camphor, and spicy, like pine. But it smelled bitter too.

"How do you feel now?" she asked after I had breathed normally a few times.

"All right. . . . I wish you'd get further away."

"Why?" she asked without moving.

"I don't—I don't want you near me. Please go further away."

Deliberately she advanced a step toward me. I gave a kind of grunt and shrank back against the wood of the chair.

"Go away," I said between my teeth.

"How do I make you feel?"

"I can't stand you. You— *Please* get away. If I could, I'd kill you. You're torturing me."

She had come closer. She was standing over me. Her face swam before my eyes.

I strained against the straps, as if I were trying to get out through the back of the chair. "Go away," I begged her desperately. "Get further off."

"If I were to touch you?"

"I'd— Don't. Don't."

She smiled very faintly. Gently she laid her small hand over mine.

It was as if she had reached through my flesh and plucked directly at my nerves. I could feel the touch running, redhot and agonizing, through my cringing body. It spared nothing. Wherever the paths of nerve impulses ran, there was pain.

I think I cried out. I was sobbing and gasping for breath. Then darkness welled up from inside my skull and covered my eyes.

When I came to, she was unbuckling the last of the straps. It seemed to me that she was paler than she had been, and that her forehead was beaded with sweat.

"How do you feel now?" she asked.

"Better. But I still wish you'd go away."

She nodded. "The drug I had you inhale," she said, "intensifies the usual repulsion people have felt toward each other since the plague. Of course it has other properties, too."

She fetched the looking glass again. "What do you see this time?" she asked as she held it in front of me.

"A fog. Now it's clearing. . . . A naked man pursued by stags."

"Where is he?"

"Behind me. In the mirror. In my head. . . . They aren't stags, they're dogs. They're catching up—"

"Who is the man?" she broke in. "Do you know him?"

"I've never seen— Yes, yes I do. He's Sam Sewell. He's myself."

"You're ready to go through, I think," she announced. She tossed the mirror over on the padded couch. "Lean on my shoulder," she said. "You'll be weaker than you expect."

She helped me out of the chair and over to the autoclave. I was as weak as if I were recovering from a long illness, and was no more ashamed to lean on her small shoulder than an invalid would have been. From her dark sleek hair a perfume, of roses and some brisker scent, came to my nose.

We stood in front of the autoclave. "Your promise," she said. "Before I put you through."

"All right. What must I promise?"

"You are going to Despoina. When you come back, you must help me up through the levels."

"To the surface?"

"Yes."

"Why don't you just go? There's nothing stopping you from going up."

She gave me an oblique glance. "There is, though. Promise you'll help."

I didn't see why I shouldn't promise. "All right, I will." She let her breath out slowly, as if she had been holding it.

She pressed on a pedal on the floor. The autoclave opened. "In with you," she said. "In the opening of the autoclave."

"In that?"

"Yes. It's not hot. Put your arms and shoulders in. I'll lift your legs."

The picture she brought up was so comic that I gave a weak chuckle. I looked at her, and sobered. She was obviously not amused.

"It's the only way out of this level that I know," she said, "and you'd be unlikely to get out that way except that I've processed you. What I did was partly physical and partly psychological. If you wait much longer, it will wear off. And then there won't be anything I can do."

"But—it's just an autoclave. A big one. But it doesn't go anywhere."

"It goes to level G. Don't argue so. Doesn't your name mean anything? You're acting like a fool."

"But—"

"The longer you wait, the more dangerous it is. Hurry! I'm not deceiving you."

She was plainly sincere. I hesitated a fraction of a second longer and then put my head and shoulders in the opening of the autoclave.

Behind me I felt her lifting my legs. For such a small girl, she was unexpectedly strong. I couldn't see anything, but there seemed to be a current of air blowing.

"Move forward with your arms!" she said. She was shoving me forward, rather as if I were a pencil she was feeding into a sharpening machine.

I obeyed. There was a tinny crash; my head seemed to have struck against something. It gave, and I felt myself sliding head downward on a steepening plane.

"Remember your promise!" she called behind me. "Keep your arms over your head and try to relax. My name's Kyra. Remember me."

I tried to make some answer, to call something. But my lungs could get no air. My body accelerated in the narrow dark.

6

A BIRD was singing. I heard the notes—metallic, repetitive, insistent—remotely for a long time before they roused me from my stupor. But at last I raised my head and sat up. I wondered where I was.

The surface under me was soft; I looked and saw grass. Over my head there was an arching tracery of branches and green leaves. I was sitting between two trees, in a sort of grove. A light, pleasant breeze ruffled my hair.

My head was aching violently; I was tempted to lie down again. Where was I? Certainly not on the surface; there are no trees there—I haven't seen a tree, let alone grass, for at least ten years. This must be level G. But how had I got here? I couldn't remember anything between Kyra's pushing me into the accelerating darkness and my hearing the song of the bird.

I turned slightly and looked around me. The motion made my head throb, and I let out a groan. The bird, which had been silent since I sat up, must have been alarmed by this. At any rate, it gave a sort of squawk and flew away. I caught a glimpse of it; it was a small, rusty-looking bird.

Yes, this must be level G. But what a spacious level, to have room spent on a grove of trees, to have birds in a sort of park! I held my head for a moment longer. Then I struggled to my feet.

I couldn't see any sign of how I had got here. The grove seemed to go on and on. The "sky" was well-lighted and blue.

I walked a few feet and then clutched at one of the trees for support. My headache was coming in waves, each more ferocious than the last. Abruptly I leaned forward and vomited.

There wasn't much in my stomach, but when I had finished I felt better. I was still holding onto the tree—some sort of birch—when I saw a girl coming toward me.

She was wearing a white blouse with ruffled puffed sleeves and a very low neckline—so low that it cleared her nipples by no more than half an inch. The lower part of her costume was a pair of extremely short, extremely tight black velvet shorts. On her feet she was wearing gilded sandals whose straps were laced about her legs halfway to her knees, in the manner of ballet slippers. It was a style of dressing I remembered having seen on the surface some ten years ago, just before the plagues began. But the necklines on the blouses had been higher then.

Her hair was a glossy black, with a flower like a red hibiscus stuck in it, and her mouth had been painted a brilliant red. There was nothing dull about her coloring, and yet, for all that, she gave an impression of something faded, like a length of cloth whose color has been bleached by time and light. Her figure was bosomy and hippy, but her knees belonged on a skinny woman.

"Hello," she said. "You've killed the grass. I saw a man do that once before. You must be from topside." She had a childish, affected way of speaking that was rather attractive and at the same time rather irritating.

I looked behind me, following the direction of her gaze. It was true, the grass where I had been lying was withered and pale. At once my fears of what I might be carrying revived,

"Keep away from me," I told her. "I'm a vector of plague."

She gave a giggle. "Don't worry about that," she said. "You couldn't infect me with anything. I've been immunized against all possible plague strains. We're important people down here, you know."

"But—I killed the grass."

She shrugged. "It's not very healthy grass anyway. You probably have some yeast spores on your clothes that bothered it. It'll be fixed. How's the war?"

"What war?" I asked blankly.

"The war that was going on when they sealed this level off, stupid. The war that started when the enemy released the spores of the plagues."

This was so different from what had actually happened that I could only stare at her. The plagues had begun near one unfortunate laboratory in Newark, had spread out across the country, killing nine people out of ten, and crossed the oceans via the airliners to Europe and the rest of the world. The "enemy" had had nothing to do with it. The latest news anybody had had of people in other countries was at least five years old, but they had been said to be suffering quite as much as we were. Presumably they had been reduced to the same sort of parasitism and disunion as we had.

"There isn't any war," I said at last.

"You mean it's been settled? Nonsense! They'd have come down and told us it was over. Or are you a spy?"

There was no use arguing with her; I felt desperate.

"I'm not a spy," I said. "I'm only trying to get through to the level below this. I'm not interested in what's going on here."

"Why do you want to go on down? It's nice here. I mean, pretty nice."

For answer, I held out Despoina's ring toward her. She looked at it critically.

"That's a funny picture," she said at last. "It must be an antique." She giggled again. "I wonder how I'd look in a dress like that."

Obviously Despoina's passport was meaningless to her. "Do you know how to get out of this level to the next lower one?" I asked.

"No; why would I? There's nothing interesting down there," she said with a pout. She pressed her thigh and shoulder against me. "I like you," she said with artificial childishness. "You're young and fresh. Different. New. I get so tired of the same old men and boys."

"Thanks. . . . Doesn't anybody on this level know how to get through to the one below?"

"I don't think so. A technician might. But there aren't any technicians down here. They aren't important people—I mean, not like us."

We had been walking along while we talked, and I found myself still somewhat shaky and uncertain. Now we came to the edge of the grove of trees. A low, large building was in front of us.

It was a handsome structure, set on a slight elevation, with broad flights of steps approaching it. It was crowned by a flattish dome. People were going up and down the steps, the women dressed in variations of the costume my guide was wearing, the men in swim trunks or bermuda snorts.

"What's that?" I asked.

"The casino. Would you like to go there first?"

"A casino? Do you have gambling here?"

"Oh, yes. Roulette, chemin de fer, chuckaluck. But it gets tiresome playing for money," she confided. "There's nothing to buy with it. So sometimes we girls play for ourselves. We stake ourselves for a month, or a week, or something like that."

"What happens if you lose?"

"Then the house disposes of us for that length of time. We have to do whatever they tell us to. It's fun."

The social activities of level G seemed to be a cloak for something not far from prostitution. Still, it wasn't any of my business. What I wanted was to get through to the level below.

"Let's skip the casino," I said.

"Well—we could go to the beach. It's a nice beach."

"A beach? Here? This far underground?"

"Oh, yes. With salt water and sand to sunbathe on. We even have tides. We're important people here, you know."

She took my hand and tugged me along childishly. She seemed to have forgotten all about her worry that I might be a spy. Her palm was warm and moist, and a little sticky.

"What's your name?" I asked as we went along a graveled path.

"Cindy Ann. Don't you think it's a pretty name? What's yours?"

"Uh-huh. Mine's Sam."

"Sam." She pronounced it with a faint lisp, so that it came out a little like Th-ham. "That's a pretty name, Th-ham."

The sand began abruptly, about ten feet ahead. We plowed across it and down to the water. As Cindy Ann had said, it was indubitably a beach, though its whole extent was no more than a hundred and fifty feet. It had a slight inward curve, and at both ends it faded into clumps of shrubbery.

"How far out does it go?" I asked.

"I don't know. It's fixed so it looks as if there were miles of water. But nobody swims out more than fifty or sixty feet."

The sand was starred with sunbathers. Their costumes were the skimpiest I have ever seen—the men wore smallish plastic fig leaves, and the women made the old joke about "two Band-Aids and a cork" seem a reasonable description. They were all nicely tanned, but somehow, like Cindy Ann, they had a faded look. As I watched them I was struck by something odd in the scene, and suddenly I realized what it was. The sunbathers lay close to each other; the people on the steps of the casino had passed near each other without apparent distaste. In short, the inhabitants of level G seemed to have an old-fashioned ability to endure each other's company.

"Cindy Ann," I said, "do you people here ever mind being near each other? Up on the surface, it bothers us to be with other people for more than a few minutes."

"I could stand being with *you* for quite a long time," she said. "Anyhow, all night."

Her amorous gestures were getting embarrassing. "Yeah. But doesn't it ever bother you?"

"Sometimes," she said more soberly. "Sometimes we have to lock ourselves in our houses away from the others for days. But usually we take a euph pill, and then we like each other again."

"A euph pill? Like a tranquillizer?"

"Oh, lots better. When you take a euph pill, you feel fine. Happy and relaxed. You like everybody, all the important people down here."

She had been holding my hand all this time. Now she turned it over and deliberately tickled my palm with her forefinger. She looked up at me inquiringly.

"What's the matter?" she asked after a moment. "Don't you feel well?"

"As a matter of fact, I don't," I answered. "My head aches, and my stomach is upset. Also, I want to get out of here."

"You need a euph pill," she said. She fumbled in the waistband of her shorts and produced an infinitesimal pillbox. She opened it and took out a tiny pink pill, which she handed to me. "Take it," she said, "and I'll have one too. You'll be surprised how good it'll make you feel."

I looked at it dubiously. But I was feeling increasingly miserable physically; the pill might help me—and I was curious. I put the pill on my tongue and washed it down with a draught of the sulphurous-smelling water from my flask.

She watched me interestedly. "We just swallow them dry," she said, "they're so small." She opened her mouth and dropped one of the tiny pills down her throat. She smiled at me. "Let's go sit in the bushes," she said.

She led me along the beach to where it faded into grass and shrubs. We walked inward until there was a wall of brush between us and the people on the beach. "Let's sit down," she said. "We can *talk*." She giggled and rolled her eyes at me.

I seated myself beside her. The euph pill must have been taking effect, for I was feeling much better. Cindy Ann seemed quite attractive—full of girlish, coltish charm.

She looked at me for a moment. Then she lay down on her side and pulled me down beside her. "Kiss me, Th-ham."

Her mouth was warm and wet. For an instant, at the contact, I felt a burst of the old separative, disjunctive repulsion; after all, I had been with her for a good many minutes now. But the euph pill was potent; I went back to kissing her.

I pulled the tail of her blouse out of the waistband of her shorts and worked the garment off over her head. She was wearing nothing under it.

Her breasts were large and only a little flabby, and by now I felt an intense, feverish desire for her. She pressed up toward me, and I took due pleasure from what she offered before I went on to the black velvet shorts. I hoped she would be wearing nothing under them, too.

She helped me with the fastening, and raised up a little so I could ease the garment down over her hips. I had got the skin-tight fabric down to the crease of her thighs when she stiffened in my arms,

She made an odd sort of noise. Her eyes rolled. Then she went limp and heavy. Her mouth dropped open and I saw a thread of green slime.

I couldn't realize at first what had happened. I called her name and shook her. Her face was flushed, and the slime had run down on her chin.

I hunted for her pulse and couldn't find any, I put my head against her chest and listened for her heart. There was no heartbeat. She was dead.

She was dead, and I was a vector of neurolytic plague. And now what was I to do? Here was a dead woman beside me. How was I to get out of level G? And how could I approach anyone for help without dooming him or her to death?

7

I BEGAN to realize that I was in a very odd physical state. My head ached, my hands and feet were cold, and I was recurrently nauseated; and the abrupt frustration of the feverish desire I had felt for Cindy Ann had left me weak and trembling. Yet simultaneously with these negative sensations, I felt that I was tall, tall enough to tower over most men like a giant, able to break a granite rock in pieces with my fingers; and that I had a double-sighted gaze.

Double-sighted? What on earth did I mean by that? I got into a comfortable position to consider the matter, with my knees under my chin and my arms linked around them. Cindy Ann lay on the ground beside me, with an increasing trickle of slime running down her chin.

Double-sighted... Well, if the word meant anything, I ought to be able to see... I fixed my eyes on the dead woman lying beside me.

It was an odd experience. Her flesh seemed to dissolve slowly as I looked. First I saw her ribs become visible, and then her lungs within the rib cage, with her motionless heart lying between them. My gaze went deeper, and then I saw her backbone and finally the grass under her. It was colored and realistic—not like an X-ray film; but the colors were rather dull.

I moved my eyes lower on her body, and the same thing happened. I noticed that one of her kidneys seemed definitely lower in her pelvis than the other, which might have caused her some trouble if she had lived.

I rubbed my eyes and looked again. The vision persisted. But it could be a hallucination, after all. I wanted to prove to myself that it wasn't that.

I looked at the waistband of her black velvet shorts. The pillbox from which she had taken the euph pill was inside a little pocket on the right side. If I reached in and found the pillbox where my double sight perceived it, it ought to prove something.

I didn't want to touch her. And besides, I'd seen her get the pillbox out of the pocket. I knew it was there already; and to find it in that spot wouldn't prove anything. I needed a more objective test.

I got to my feet and looked around me. There was a tallish tree a few feet ahead of me, and I tried my double sight on it.

Seeing the bark dissolve and the tree's woody anatomy become visible wasn't interesting. I moved my eyes to a crotch in the tree's trunk and was rewarded by seeing, quite hidden from my ordinary sight by the sides of the crotch, a bird's nest slowly become visible. The nest, built down deep in the hollow, contained four naked young.

It ought to be easy enough to check up on a thing like that. I caught hold of a horizontal branch and pulled myself up to the level of the crotch. The effort was unpleasant; I might be able to break a piece of granite with my fingers, but I wasn't able to chin myself without feeling woozy. But, before I let go of the branch and dropped back to the ground, I saw a nest with four naked, snaky-necked baby birds in it. They cheeped loudly at me.

It wasn't a hallucination, then. But it might be an elaborate dream—or a systematized series of delusions. . . . Nonsense. I was in a peculiar physical condition; some extremely odd things were happening in me. But I wasn't dreaming, and I wasn't deluded. The faculty my mind had elected to call "double sight" really existed in me. How could I use it to help myself?

I sat down on the ground again by Cindy Ann's body to think it over. Proximity to her didn't bother me at all. It was like sitting down by an empty packing case, or a bundle of old clothes. I suppose it was because I didn't have any feeling of moral responsibility for her death. And then, she hadn't had much personality when she had been alive. Not much had been withdrawn.

Ames had called Despoina's ring a passport to get me past the guards on the lower levels. I had assumed, without even thinking about it, that when he had said "guards" he had meant "guardians." Certainly that was what Kyra, on level F, had seemed to be. But the word "guard" has another meaning. One speaks, for example, of a chain guard on a bicycle, or of a mud guard on an automobile. Had Ames meant to employ the word in this second sense also? In that case, the "guard" on this level might be a piece of machinery that Despoina's ring would activate—or inactivate.

There was another thing. Ames had said Despoina meant me to go to her. In that case, might there not be some cooperation to be expected from her, or from her agents? Would she not help me to get to her?

I raised the ring to my eyes and looked at it. I looked at it for what seemed a long time. I could see my hand through the ring, and the bones inside it. But that was all that happened.

At last I sighed and got to my feet. The best thing I could think of was to wander through level G looking at things and people with my double sight. I didn't think I'd infect anyone by merely walking through the level. After all, Cindy Ann had had to be in close physical contact with me before I had infected her.

Where should I go first? To the casino? It seemed an unlikely place, somehow, to find a level "guardian." (If I did find one, would I be able to recognize him—or her? Would my double sight be of any help to me?) I'd walk back the way Cindy Ann and I had come, to the place in the grove where I had landed on level G, and see what lay on the other side of it.

It took me five minutes or so to get back to the spot in the grove where the withered grass was. Kyra had hinted that my perception of time was disturbed, and it may have been longer. Before I left the grove entirely, I crossed a little brook that rippled pleasantly along over pebbles and sand. A brook, at this depth! They did things handsomely on level G.

Beyond the grove were random groups of dwelling houses. Each one was set among trees and shrubbery, and, while they seemed a little smaller than houses of comparable luxury would have been on the surface, they were all of good size. Now and then I saw people going in and out of them.

Nobody paid much attention to me, though one or two women eyed me speculatively. One of them even nodded and smiled, and I nodded back. Obviously, she thought she knew me. I suppose the explanation is that I have always had an ordinary, or perhaps the more accurate word would be a plastic face. When I was growing up, the other youngsters had teased me because I was so hard to locate in a group photograph. Here on level G, despite my shirt and trousers, I looked like anybody else.

I soon found that Cindy Ann's costume had been rather conservative. Two of the women that I passed had blouses cut so low that their naked breasts were entirely exposed, and the women were by no means the youngest or the prettiest of those who sauntered along the graveled walks.

No matter who I passed, man or woman, I looked at him or her with my double sight. I saw a lot of human anatomy, and might, had I been interested, have learned a lot of visceral secrets. But I saw nobody who seemed to me likely to be one of the putative "guardians."

I passed through a heavy belt of trees and then came to a sort of shopping center. Cindy Ann had said that they didn't use money: but people were going in and out of several shops and coming out with packages of frozen foods and what looked like wrapped-up clothing. One of the shops seemed to be a pharmacy. Nowhere did I see a salesperson or an attendant. I suppose the constructors of level G had thought its amenities too good to waste on anyone who wasn't an "important" person. But, despite Cindy Ann's denial, there must be a technician or two somewhere on this level, after all, if only to keep its complex machines running. There is a limit to what the best-constructed robot can do.

I didn't enter any of the shops—I was afraid of being recognized as an outsider, since I wouldn't know what the procedure was for getting goods. I walked as slowly as I dared, and tried to inspect everyone inside.

The "shopping center" gave place to another belt of trees, and this to more houses. As I walked along, I thought how inexhaustible the supply of goods on level G must be. Some of the people I saw must have come down here when they were children, when the danger of war had seemed so agonizingly immediate. They had grown into young men and women, the plagues had raged on the surface, and still people entered the shops and brought out parcels. They had been prepared to live underground for a quarter or half a century; the material wealth of a culture had been poured out to make them safe and happy. If they were bored, they could always take a euph pill.

And how enormous the level was! The trees could be justified, on the ground that their leaves helped keep the atmosphere breathable, and that their trunks served to hide the steel girders that supported the levels above. But a brook... private dwelling houses... a casino... and even a most realistic bathing beach—only space to spare could account for it. I had read somewhere, years ago, that excavating the levels had cost $300,000 for each cubic foot of earth removed.

Big as the level was, still it was not unlimited. Sooner or later I must come to where shrubbery and illusion gave place to the native rock.

At last I reached the edge of the second constellation of houses. There was another belt of trees, a trailing out of shrubbery and flowering plants. The path I had been following came to an end. I saw the bare gray rock before me. And close against it, small and unexpected, a house.

Small, and, if not quite dilapidated, certainly not very well kept up. The window frames needed painting, the boards of the porch seemed to sag a trifle. Probably prefabricated, I thought. The ivy vines that were growing in clay flower pots had a discouraged look. Who would be living, on level G, in a house like this?

Oh, but it was obvious. The technician Cindy Ann had said didn't exist, and that I had been sure must be here.

Without even thinking, I walked up the two porch steps and knocked on the door.

There was a wait. I heard somebody moving inside. I knocked again. At last a woman came to the door.

She did not open it very wide. Her body stayed inside, and only her face peeped out.

She was middle-aged, with a dusky skin and an intelligent, strong, impetuous face. "Who is it?" she asked warily.

I had been thinking of what to say. Now words deserted me. I held out my hand to her, so she could see Despoina's ring.

She shot me a startled glance. "I don't know anything about it!" she said vehemently. "I don't know anything about it at all, no more than if I was a *dog!*" She slammed the door in my face.

I knocked again. For quite a long while I kept on knocking. But she did not come back.

At last I turned away. ". . . no more than if I was a *dog.*" What had she meant by that?

It occurred to me, with the sense of a wasted opportunity, that I had not used my double sight on her. But perhaps there had been nothing to see anyway.

I started walking again. For a while I kept close to the rock wall. The going was not easy, because of the piles of loose rubble and the knee-high, slanting steel supporting members I had to detour around. But it seemed to me that here, close to the edge of the excavation, was a logical place for the exit from G to the next level below to be.

I found nothing. I was getting tired, and had just about decided to abandon my tour of the periphery of G for the center, where walking would be easier, when I saw before me a flash of familiar color. I got up to it, and it was what I had thought it was. A patch of the purple fungus was growing there.

I don't know why, but I felt heartened. For one thing, the sight of the fungus made me realize I was hungry. I fished my knife from my pocket and cut off a handful of the crisp, succulent fronds. I chewed them slowly, leaning against the rough face of the raw rock, and they tasted good. They were the first thing I had had to eat in a long time—actually, as I realized later, the first thing in several days. I washed the fungus down with a drink, from my flask, of the sulphurous water I had got on level F.

As I corked the flask, I thought of Kyra. Her playing with the knife came into my mind, and I wondered what she had meant by it. Then I started out along the rock wall once more.

Still nothing. One heap of rock rubble looked exactly like another. I kept on stubbornly, but at last I realized I was too tired to walk much longer. I decided to head back to the center of G, to see if I could find a place to rest.

When I think of G now, it is always in terms of endless walking. I was tired, so tired I could hardly put one foot in front of the other, and my awareness of my surroundings grew hazier and hazier.

At last I stopped. I was in another of the groves of trees, somewhere, I thought, not far from the casino and the little beach. This was as good a place as any to rest. I didn't think anybody would find me here, unless a pair of lovers stumbled on me by accident. Anyhow, I had to have rest.

I threw myself down on the grass. I promised myself that after I had slept for a while I would resume the hunt for the exit. . . . After I had slept.

I was asleep almost as soon as I lay down. My dreams slid into a deep unconsciousness, a profound and gratifying oblivion. I sank to the bottom of a sea of welcome nothingness.

At last I began to come to the surface again. Something was rubbing against my cheek, and I moved to avoid it. Still it kept on, gentle and persistent.

After a long time, I opened my eyes. I was still unwilling to awake, but I had begun to be curious. What was it that returned, over and over again, to rubbing my cheek?

I blinked, yawned, and then I laughed. A big reddish-brown setter, glossy-coated and handsome, was standing over me. Even while I lay there, the dog's red tongue came out again and licked insistently at my cheek.

8

HE WAS wearing a collar. His name was engraved on it—Dekker, it was. I thought it an odd name for a dog.

I sat fondling him and smiling, it was so long since I had seen a dog. I pulled his silky ears and he wagged his tail amiably.

He sat down facing me, grinning, his red tongue lapping out. Wobblingly, I got to my feet. My nap had unquestionably done me good—I felt stronger and steadier, and my headache had gone. At the same time, the physical changes in me had progressed further than before. The skin of my whole body felt glowingly warm, and unless I held my head perfectly still objects around me rotated dizzyingly. The mere exertion of getting to my feet had left me drenched with sweat.

Dekker, sitting before me, gave a faint whine. For the first time I looked at him with my double sight.

His body, so far as I could tell, was a perfectly normal canine body. It would have done for an illustration in a textbook called "The Anatomy of the Dog." But his head seemed different. It was harder to see into, and when I did get through the opacity of the bone I was puzzled. I couldn't make sense of what I saw.

I peered intently, hardly breathing. And then I realized, with a deep tingling of the spirit, that he had a double brain.

Double sight, and double brain? Yes. Above the normal mammalian two hemispheres, he had another smaller structure, one-lobed and deeply convoluted. It was not a tumor or any diseased creation; it was a double brain.

I drew an astonished breath. Was a dog, then, the guardian of the exit from this level? I knew that I was in an abnormal physical condition; perhaps my coming up with such an idea indicated only how abnormal my condition was.

Dekker had stopped grinning while I looked at him. Now he stood up, shook himself briskly, and started trotting away from me. After he had gone a few feet he stopped and looked over his shoulder at me. He gave a short bark. Plainly, he wanted me to follow him.

He led me to the beach. It was still dotted with bathers; the "sun" was as high as ever. Turning now and then to be sure I was following him, he galloped across the sand until he found a stick, a length of dried branch. He raced back with it in his mouth, and dropped it at my feet. He wanted me to play with him.

For a moment I had a painfully let-down feeling. A dog, who might or might not have something wrong with his head, wanted to have a game of stick-throwing with an amiable stranger. Was this why he had awakened me, and insisted I follow him to the beach? So I would throw a stick for him?

Standing over the stick, he barked peremptorily. Well, it wouldn't do any harm to play with a dog. Creakily I picked up the stick and tossed it.

He galloped off after it enthusiastically, scattering sand over one or two of the sunbathers. One girl rolled over on her stomach, away from him. They all seemed to know him and find nothing unusual in his playing a game of stick.

Twice more I threw the stick for him and he returned it. The fourth time, when I bent over to pick it up, he growled at me.

I straightened up, feeling annoyed. I had only been playing with the animal because I couldn't think of anything better to do. And now I got growled at for my pains.

Dekker looked from me to the water and back to me again. Oh, that was it. I was supposed to throw the stick in the water. He'd retrieve it. But what a waste of time! And a nuisance, too, since every time I bent over I was unpleasantly giddy. With no enthusiasm at all, I threw the stick in the water for him.

It landed beyond the edge of the gentle surf and floated quietly, bobbing up and down a little. He dashed in after it, swam out to where it was, and returned it to my feet. He was dripping wet and, as I bent over to pick up the stick, he shook salt water all over me.

He was as brainless as a spaniel. I threw the stick once more, resolved that this should be the last time.

It landed ten feet or so from where I had thrown it before. Dekker looked toward it and then squatted down on his haunches.

"Go on," I said. "Bring it here."

He made no move to retrieve it, but his eyes turned from the stick to me, and back again.

"Get it, old boy," I ordered again. "Go after it."

Deliberately he got up, turned around, and sat down with his back to me, so he could see the water.

The action had so much of purpose in it that, despite my current low estimation of Dekker's intelligence, I looked out over the water to where he seemed to want me to look.

The stick I had thrown was bobbing up and down in the water, but it also had another motion. It was moving strongly and steadily to the right.

Was there a current there? Was that what the dog had wanted me to see?

I watched intently, while the dog squatted near me. The stick reached a certain point in its rightward motion and then began to move straight out, away from the beach. Faster and faster it moved. Then, when it seemed to be perhaps a hundred and fifty feet out, it disappeared. I couldn't tell whether I had merely lost sight of it, or whether it had actually gone.

Gone? Gone where? Cindy Ann had said nobody swam out further than fifty or sixty feet, though the water looked as if it extended for miles. Where was there for the stick to go? Presumably the beach was an extremely large saltwater swimming pool, with cunningly contrived machinery that kept the waves coming in, and even, at certain times, caused high or low tides. But it did not seem that machinery to do *that* would cause the effect of outward suction I had seen. What had become of the stick?

Dekker looked up at me. When he saw he had my attention, he ran along the beach, hunted, and returned with another stick. It seemed he wanted me to throw this one into the water, too.

Obligingly, I threw, trying to make it land where the other stick had landed. Once more the sequence of motion was repeated—to the right, and then the rapid motion away from the beach. And, again, at a certain point the stick disappeared.

I tried to use my double sight to see through the water, to find if there was any machinery that would account for the motion I had observed. After a few feet, though, my special sight was not much more use than ordinary vision was. I had an impression of turbulence, of greenish water falling. That was all.

My game with the dog had tired me. Sweat was trickling along my face and dripping off the point of my chin. I was as wet with sweat as if I had been in a bath, and yet my body felt hotter than ever.

I sat down in the sand to think. Dekker lay down beside me quietly, his head on my knee. . . . What had made the sticks move like that?

No. That wasn't the real question. The question was why Dekker had wanted me to notice it.

Had he only been playing? Perhaps; and yet his actions seemed too purposeful. There was some reason why he wanted me to witness the outward motion and the final disappearance of the sticks.

He had been lying quietly beside me. Now he stood up and put his nose under my outstretched hand and snuggled his head under it.

I thought at first he wanted me to fondle him, and I rubbed his big red-brown head absently behind the ears. But that wasn't it; he walked out from under my hand and stood as if he were thinking. Then he took my wrist gently between his big jaws and came close to me, so my arm had to bend at the elbow. He put his paws up on my thighs and held my hand in front of my face.

I looked at my hand. An ordinary hand, except that it was so hot. But on the finger—Despoina's ring. That was what he had wanted me to see.

Suddenly I understood. The place where the sticks had disappeared was the exit from level G. The dog had been showing me how to get out of it.

"Dekker. . ." I said.

He had dropped my wrist and was watching me motionlessly. He scarcely seemed to breathe. Through his skull I could see the strange second brain above his normal canine brain.

"Dekker, is that the way out of this level? Where the sticks moved out?"

Dogs don't nod their heads; he gave a short, decisive bark.

It sounded exactly like "Yes." Still I hesitated. I am only a moderately good swimmer, and even if what Dekker seemed to be telling me actually was the case, I was afraid the outward current might sweep me into some machinery I would have trouble coping with. I didn't suppose there was an actual flow of water from this level into the one below, so that I would only have to let myself be swept along with it.

Dekker sighed, the impatient sigh of a dog who has been waiting a long time for his master to be done reading and go for a walk with him. Then he caught my trouser leg by the cuff and gave me a tug in the direction of the water.

I laughed and stood up. Yes, he had been patient. "Okay, boy," I said. "I'll get going."

We walked over the sand together and out into the water. It can't have been very usual for people to go in swimming fully dressed, but nobody on the beach paid any attention to me. Probably they thought I was drunk, if they thought about it at all. Their curiosity seemed to have atrophied along with the rest of their personalities.

When I got out far enough I started swimming, and Dekker swam along beside me. I think the water would have felt good, if I had not been so feverish. As it was, it seemed chillingly cold.

We swam out together for what seemed a long way. I was interested to find that even at this distance from the beach the illusion of unlimited space continued, though I could see that there was some sort of wall ahead.

Suddenly Dekker, who was on my left, turned and swam against me, so I was forced to the right. "Is this the place, old fellow?" I asked. He managed a muffled bark.

I swam in the direction he had pushed me. After a little while I found a gentle current toward the right, and realized I was moving just as the sticks had done. I was glad of the current, since my arms had grown exceedingly tired.

Dekker did not go with me. He stayed where he had been when he pushed me, paddling a little and looking toward me.

I waved my hand toward him; he was so human that it seemed only natural to say good-bye. Then the current changed direction and set in much more strongly. I knew I was being borne straight on out.

Toward what? The rock wall was near now. The illusion of space had vanished. I could see the paint on the wall and the layers and puffs of gauze in front of it.

Abruptly I was borne down. Half-consciously I must have been expecting this, and I did not fight against it. It would have done me no good if I had; the downward pull was irresistible. It was as if a giant hand had taken hold of my legs.

The wave closed over my head. I was in a green, rushing world. There was a roaring in my ears. Down and down and down.

Ahead of me I saw a spot of light.

9

"HORSE, HORSE and hattock!" I cried. "And away!" I threw my leg over the pole with the curiously carved end, neighed like a horse, and began to prance and cavort around the smoke-streaked blaze of the bonfire.

The others mounted too, and followed. Nearer and nearer to the fire we went, spiraling inward, until at last I plucked the pole from between my legs, balanced an instant, and leaped straight over the fire.

I felt the heat as I went over, and then the cool rush of the night air. There was a shout of approval, and the others began shooting over the flames, flying like birds, the girls no less bravely than the men. They gave the old cries as they went, long and thrilling, and I thought, "The wheat will grow tall this year."

I straddled my pole again and went dancing off, unwinding the spiral. But the light of the fire was too bright; even as I moved away from it, it seemed to get brighter, and I felt frightened. Frightened? In the happy night, around our leaping sun-fire? But my heart was thudding, and the fire grew brighter.

The light was pitiless, a stony glare that defeated the kindly shadows. I tried to hide my head from it under the crook of my elbow, to burrow through the rock back into darkness. In vain. It struck through my eyelids insistently. I was impaled on the hard light.

At last I opened my eyes. The light was not the hard glare it had seemed in my dream, but bright enough, and absolutely shadowless. It was the illumination of the operating room.

I tried to sit up. For the first time it came to me that my disease—there was no other word for it—my disease had progressed to the point where not only my perceptions were unreliable, but my thoughts about my perceptions were untrustworthy too. Well, there wasn't much I could do about it.

I was lying on a little rise with my back to the rock wall and the intense shadowless light all about me. The rock ceiling was low, and the space before me was not very big, say twenty by twenty feet. There was a rectangular doorway in the rock at the end of it.

I propped myself up on one arm. The movement made the scene swing around me, and I saw clouds coming out of it. When I held my head still, the clouds—dark blue-gray, and puffy—went back into the rock.

I looked down at myself. I was still wearing paper shirt and trousers, but my shoes had disappeared. My clothing was dry, except for the hems of my trousers. They were still a little wet.

What had happened to my shoes? How had I got here? I remembered swimming toward the spot of light, reaching it, and seeming to be borne abruptly *upward,* I had swum for dear life in a rushing confusion of waters, snatching a breath when the wild cross-threshing would allow me, and swallowing a lot of water. Then I had been washed up—or down; by then I had been buffeted about until I had lost all sense of direction—on a hard wooden surface.

It had been almost dark; I had felt about with my hands. I had seemed to be in some sort of cage. Then the cage had begun to descend.

What had happened after that? I couldn't remember. I might have gone to sleep. I had a dim recollection of having been catapulted out of the cage at some point, and landing on a surface of springy balsam boughs. That might have been a dream. But there was nothing in what I could remember to account for the loss of my shoes.

I tried to get to my feet. Lord, how ill I felt! My bones ached as if they were breaking, and my chest felt as if it were a hollow that had been scooped through to my backbone. My skin felt red-hot. My double sight had gone completely. Indeed, it was an effort for me to hold the objects around me in any sort of focus. If I relaxed, they blurred and swam.

For a moment I lay back on the unyielding rock. If I just stayed here, what would happen? But I hadn't made my way down through the levels to lie on bare rock while fever consumed me. I had come down to find—

I managed to get my hand up before my eyes and look at it. Yes, the ring was still there.

Without any warning I began to shiver violently. I shook so hard my teeth clicked together and my legs jerked wildly on the rock. Then the fit passed and my skin began to burn again.

I got my flask out and unstoppered it. The water inside was warm and sulphurous, but I emptied the flask. After I had drunk I felt a little better; sweat broke out and cooled my skin, and for a moment I was almost comfortable. My flashlight and knife were gone.

I got to my knees, and then into a half-erect crouch. At the foot of the little rise there was a map of the world, carte du monde, mappamondo, karte der welt, with the countries marked on it in brilliant colors. I knew that if I wanted to go anywhere, from Angola to Paphlagonia, all I had to do was to put my foot on the spot. The kingdoms of the world and the glory thereof. Or was that something I had read in a book?

I got to the bottom of the little slope, and there was nothing there but a few spots and patches, natural discolorations of the rock. I stumbled toward the doorway, and a man came out of the rock and stood in front of me. There was a flame thrower in his hands.

He was dressed in a dark gray, shiny cloth that clung to his thighs and chest in great folds. His face was hidden by a dark gray mask with a pendant chin cloth. I saw him with extraordinary sharpness, but as if I were looking at him through the wrong end of an opera glass.

I held up my hand so he could see Despoina's ring. He nodded, lowered the flame thrower, and wheeled back into the rock.

I got through the rectangular doorway. Here, in a narrow space like a hallway, there were five doorways side by side, all facing me.

Which one should I enter? While I stood hesitating, five men came out of the rock and leveled flame throwers at me.

"Which way shall I go?" I asked, but they did not answer. They stepped forward menacingly, and I had to show them the ring to make them go back in the rock.

Then I was free to go forward, but which door should I choose? "The cuckoo's nest!" I cried, and stumbled through the middle door.

Here for a moment it seemed dark, and then I realized it was as light as anywhere else. Walls and floor were suffused with the same constant, wearisome, shadowless light.

I was in a long corridor. I made my way along it, stopping now and then to lean against the wall and rest. Once while I was resting a toad popped out of a hole and looked at me. When he saw my ring, "Pass that by!" he said.

Now a great bank of guns swung toward me. The mouths were open, ready to belch out shells. I wondered how there was room in the corridor for all that width. I knew that even if I lay on my belly, the shells would reach me. I saw my spine lying exposed, like the backbone of a sardine. But I held up Despoina's ring, and the guns slid by.

Later, I wondered how much of this had been real. Men do not step out of solid rock, of course, and the bank of guns had been too wide for the corridor. But level H had been designed as the last redoubt for what was considered, at the time it was built, the most precious life in the country. It is reasonable to think that it did, in fact, conceal much elaborate weaponry. The people I ask about this either do not know, or will not say.

The rock corridor kept turning corners. Twice more I was confronted with five doors, and each time I had to make my choice.

Then abruptly the rock floor gave way under my feet and I fell down a flight of steps. Here it ought to have been dark, but it was, like everywhere else here, mercilessly light. No matter how tightly I shut my eyes I could still see the shadowless light.

My ears felt odd. It seemed I had suddenly gone much more deeply into the earth. I was thirsty, but the water in my flask was all gone. Also, I felt a little hunger. But it was not reasonable to think that the purple fungus would grow on rock that was so bathed in light. I never did find any of it.

There were black moments, of course. Sometimes I would feel the blood draining from my eyes, and darkness covering me. Or I would move forward and find I had stumbled on in a mist of semi-consciousness. These times were not unwelcome to me; they were a refuge from too much light. But always the light beat against my eyes until I took up the burden of shadowless noon again.

I don't know how long I wandered. Later, from the evidence, I think it must have been for at least two days. Much of the time I retraced my steps and followed the bends of the labyrinth. There was nothing direct or steady in my progress. But at last I came to a door.

A door, not a doorway. As I lurched toward it an arc of steel blades sprang into being around it, crossed like plaited thorns, aimed at my chest.

It expanded out toward me, menace flashing from the bright tips of the blades. A mazy crown, a warlike blossoming. Who gathered the flowers, and who wove such a wreath?

I backed away from it, stumbling into the walls of the corridor and backing away again. The arc of steel followed me, until at last the blades grew misty and dissolved.

I stood rocking on my feet and shaking my head. I ought to have shown it the ring. At last I took a tentative step forward. Somebody threw a hand grenade at me.

I am inclined to think the grenade was real. It exploded with a deafening sound in the enclosed space, made louder by the rocky floor and walls—much too loud a sound to have been an auditory hallucination. Also, the rocky chips it threw up cut my arms and chest, and I found the cuts on them afterward. Yes, the grenade was real. It did not kill me because I was so far back in the corridor.

I had thrown up my arms to protect my face when I saw the grenade coming. As the sound of the explosion died away, and the rock dust settled, I lurched forward, my clenched fist held in front of me. That was so the ring on it could be seen.

I reached the door. Nothing happened. I turned the door knob, and went in.

It might have been booby-trapped, but it wasn't. I had enough normal caution left to be worried. But nothing happened.

I was in a small room, an office, with a big desk bearing a battery of telephones, a built-in bunk, and a washbasin at the side. There was an American flag over the desk, but it had come loose at one corner and sagged over itself. The edges of the flag were tattered. In the space it had once covered somebody had drawn, on the bare rock, the sign of the double axe.

I picked up one of the telephones. I heard a sort of buzzing, but I think it was illusory. Nobody was at the other end, nobody ever would be. None of the bells of the telephones would ever ring.

I sat down in the desk chair. The light in the office was a normal light, not the pitiless glare that lit the rest of level H. For a moment my mind steadied, and I realized where I was.

This was the holy of holies, the heart of level H. I had come to the innermost spot. And there was nothing there.

10

A ROUND glass paperweight lay on the desk. A disk of glass, with rounded edges, and the green of the clean blotting paper showed through it. I picked it up and looked at it.

For a long time nothing happened. Then the glass clouded and I saw a scene, unclear, with many figures moving against a wintry darkness, while, raised a few feet above them, there was a red glow and a smoky flickering. For a reason I did not then understand, the picture filled me with great dread, and I dropped the paperweight with shaking fingers.

I realized that I was thirsty. I levered myself up out of the desk chair, while the room wheeled about me and the floor seemed ready to slide out from under my feet. But I held on to the desk chair, and worked myself over to the washbasin. Here I got a paper cup from a dispenser on the wall, held it under the tap, and turned the faucet.

Water came out in a thin, grudging stream. It had a faintly greenish tinge, as if algae grew in it. But it was water, and tasted good. I filled the cup four or five times before I threw it away.

I looked at the bunk. Why not? Wherever I was going, it seemed to me I had got there, and I was dead tired as well as sick. I threw myself down on it.

It was well sprung, as was appropriate for the chief executive's bed. "Commander in chief of the army and navy . . . with the advice and consent . . ." I fell like a stone into the depths of sleep.

I slept for a very long time. What woke me was something whose oddness may not be immediately apparent: the room was dark.

You cannot imagine how odd it was. For days, ever since I had spent the night in the rock cleft under the labrys sign, under the double axe, I had lived in constant bright light. And now there was darkness. No wonder it had wakened me.

I had no trouble remembering where I was. My fever had gone completely and left me clammy and shivering, filled with a cold lassitude. I didn't want to move, and saw no reason why I should move.

I seemed perfectly clear-headed, but I had the impression that my consciousness had become detached from my body. It was hovering in the air just at the level of my head and about two feet to the right, watching, without much interest, whatever I might or might not do. Actually, I think my mental disorientation reached its maximum about this time. I no longer had the overt hallucinations of high fever, but my mind mingled present, past, remote past, and even some premonitions of the future without recognizing any difference between them. Everything was "now."

What finally made me rouse myself was a faint feeling of curiosity. The room was dark now; that meant somebody must have turned the light off. Who? Why? Did I still have the ring?

I felt my hand, and was relieved that the circlet was still there. I lay a while longer, and then decided to get up. It was then that I discovered that my feet were bound.

Not tied to the bunk, but bound together. I felt over the ropes as well as I could in the darkness—the room was utterly black—and tried to loosen them. But they had been well tied, with the knots I was later to recognize as traditional, and I made no impression on them. I had lost my pocketknife long ago.

I didn't feel frightened, only curious. It seemed to me this had happened before. I swung my legs over the edge of the bunk and got to my feet. Then, after orienting myself with reference to the bunk, I hopped toward the door.

It was hard work, but possible. Again, I had the impression of familiarity. When I reached the door I opened it, and stood looking out into the corridor.

It, too, was dark. Not as utterly dark as the office had been—I could see a faint, faint glimmering, the worn-out ghost of light, ahead.

I clutched the door knob to support myself. I leaned outward, listening intently, and I may have heard, a long way off, a tiny scurrying. That was all.

Where should I go now? What should I do? Surely I had come to the bottom of everything! Then came a twitch on the rope that bound my feet. A tug, a twitch. It was as if somebody had decided that at last the period of wandering was over, and I had better come straight on.

I hesitated. The tug was repeated. I began to hop in the direction I was being pulled.

Hopping is an exhausting method of progression. I had to keep stopping to rest. When I did that, the tug would be repeated, and I would hop on.

I could not tell where I was going, of course. Sometimes I seemed to turn corners, and once it even seemed that I hopped back where I had been. But I had a sense of steady downward motion. The pressure in my ears told me I was going deeper. I had not come to the bottom of level H, then; it was deeper than I had thought.

I was leaning against the wall, panting, when a darker shadow moved in front of me. It was a man, wearing a long cowled robe. The cowl was drawn over his head, hiding it. I felt an extraordinary terror at the sight.

"The hound!" I heard myself saying faintly. And then I clapped my hand over my mouth to silence the betraying cry.

The shadow disappeared, and once more I felt the tug.

It was getting cold. I could feel an icy chill striking up through the soles of my feet. It was as if I hopped over a sheet of ice. Then I took an incautious hop onward, slipped on the glassy surface, and spilled forward onto my hands. As I writhed upright again, I realized that the surface over which I moved actually *was* ice. I had gone deep enough that I was hopping over a sort of river of ice.

And now, trees. Darker shadows that I hopped through neatly, obedient to the tug at my feet. Once or twice I became aware that they were not trees at all, but great pillars, partly hewn and partly natural, that supported the roof. But I soon went back to thinking of them as trees again.

It was just a little lighter now than it had been. Despite this advantage, I missed my footing again, and this time took a fall on my back. I couldn't catch myself, and went rolling over and over, until I came to rest, winded and bruised, against one of the stone tree trunks.

Here I lay for a considerable time. When I once stopped moving, a great lassitude invaded me. There were many monitory twitches of the rope that bound my feet, before I at last inched and jackknifed myself upright and stood again on my hobbled feet.

I had made not more than four hops forward when a man stepped out from behind one of the groined trunks and stood facing me.

He had the head of a stag, with great sweeping horns—it was a mask, of course—and he was entirely naked except for a band of leather just under his right knee. His hands were held behind his back.

"Which hand will you have?" he asked me in a deep, hoarse voice.

"The left," I answered unhesitatingly. It seemed to me that this had happened before, and that my response was given in accordance with a familiar rule. Indeed it was, though it was not a rule I had learned during Sam Sewell's life.

Silently the man in the mask tore open my shirt so that my breast was bare. Then, with a surgeon's precision, he laid his fingers just over my heart.

His hand was unbelievably cold. A chill came from it that reached through the walls of my chest and struck inward to my heart. It was as if he squeezed it in great icy fingers. I could feel it leap like a horse and then try bravely to keep on beating against the pressure and the cold.

"Who are you?" I asked faintly with my scanty breath.

"The lord of the gates of death. And life."

He took his hand away. I felt the blood flowing back, and my heart, still giving great leaps, began to beat in its rhythm again.

"Now you must know the pangs."

As he spoke, he brought his right hand forward, and I saw he had a three-thonged scourge in it. For a moment he crossed his arms over his breast, with his hands touching his shoulders. Then he raised the whip and struck me viciously with it.

I think I cried out. It was not the pain, but another horror, as if the blows of the scourge threatened something more vital than my body. The blows were like white fire, impalpable and spiritual. Some will know what I mean.

I staggered under the lashing, and tried to hop forward. I could not move, and he lashed me relentlessly, until at last I cried, "I know! I know!"

At this he nodded. He crossed his arms once more on his breast. "Blessed be," he said. He walked around behind one of the tree trunks, and disappeared.

I stood shuddering, waiting for the tug on my bonds to be renewed. No impulse came, and after a while I began to hop forward again. It seemed to me that ahead there was just a faint lightening of the dark.

Yes. It was no illusion. I hopped forward painfully, and after a while, I saw an unmistakable twinkling light.

It happened abruptly. One moment I was still in the forest of pillars. The next I stood in a little open space. And I saw Despoina there.

Despoina, the long-sought. It was certainly she. She stood before a rock wall heavily overgrown with the purple fungus, so that it was like a tapestry. She wore the costume of the woman in the gem.

Her molten-copper hair hung loose over her shoulders, and the whiteness of her body was dazzling. Two candles burned at her feet, and on either side of her a lion crouched. Then one of them moved, and I saw that they were masked men.

Yes, Despoina. For her I had gone deep and wandered painfully. Her ring had been my passport, her name had been my lodestar. And now that I stood before her, I felt nothing at all.

I hopped toward her on my hobbled feet. She neither moved nor spoke. I took the ring off my hand and held it out to her. At this final moment, I felt like a man delivering a telegram.

Her face did not change. She took the ring from me and slipped it over her finger. And suddenly, as if her action had released something frozen in me, my indifference was gone.

I looked at her with fresh, astonished eyes. It was as if I had just been born, and she was the first being I had ever seen. I felt an extraordinary freshness and delight.

The twinkling of the tapers seemed to fill the air with a tiny joyous dust of stars, a laughter of little sparks. They burned in trails of gold, through which I saw Despoina's faintly smiling face.

"Blessed be my feet," I said, "that have brought me in these ways."

One of the lion-headed men bent forward and worked briefly at the ropes around my ankles. They fell away easily and left me standing in a circle of cord.

"Blessed be thy feet," Despoina responded gravely. They were the first words I had heard her speak; and her voice, soft and low, filled me with the same astonished pleasure that the scene about me did. Her eyes had begun to shine.

"Blessed be my eyes," I said, "that have looked on the Lady."

"Blessed be thy eyes." Her voice lifted a little, in a half-caress. Once more I felt that shock of delight.

"Blessed be my mouth, that will tas—"

There was a deep, grinding roar from among the pillars at my left. Despoina's head jerked round and, as I followed her gaze, I saw the distant rock walls slide in grooves, like paper screens.

I must have been in a highly labile, precariously balanced state of consciousness. For, as I saw the solid walls moving, the real scene around me was blotted out, and I saw a great wave of fire well up.

It burned with terrible brightness, as if sulphur had been mixed in it. There was none of the kindly, stupefying smoke, only the horrible clear fire.

"The drugs!" I cried in anguish. "You promised! I trusted you! I went steadfast to the flames!"

Nobody answered. I screamed again. The fire was lapping at my face, and I tried wildly to push it away from me.

Darkness rushed down on me, and a baking heat. I fell among gold masks.

11

My RETURN to awareness was entirely classical. That is, for a long time before I opened my eyes I was remotely aware of somebody who gave me water to sip, smoothed my bed, and performed other less seemly services for me. There were times when I almost roused myself, but always I slipped back into unconsciousness again.

But at last I got my eyes open and kept them open. The room was only dimly lighted, but I could see someone sitting in a chair against the wall. I asked the classical question. "Where am I?" I said.

The woman got up and came over to my bedside. "Well," she said, "so you've come to at last. You certainly took your time about it."

It was Kyra. And even with my still blurry vision I could see that she looked tired and worn.

"Where am I?" I asked again.

"On level F. In my rooms."

"Have I been here long?"

"About ten days. You've been a handful. Heavy, too."

"How did I get here?"

"Don't ask so many questions. You're still weak. Go on back to sleep, and I'll go in the room next door and do some sleeping on my own hook."

"But—"

"Don't argue. I know what's best for you." She gave me a severe look and walked away. I heard the door close.

Something in her roughness and lack of courtesy made me feel remarkably secure. I managed a faint chuckle. I rolled over on my side and slid into deep, restful sleep.

I was awakened, a long time later, by Kyra touching my shoulder. "Suppertime," she said. She looked much more rested than she had before.

She slipped an arm under my shoulders, raised me up, and deftly punched the pillows into a back rest. Then she brought a tray with a dish of food on it. "Shall I help you eat?" she asked.

"I don't think so," I said. "I can manage a fork."

"Okay." She sat down opposite me and began her own meal.

What she had brought me was a dish of the purple fungus, stewed with beef cubes and dehydrated onions. It was not what I would have thought of as invalid food, but it tasted good. I emptied the dish and could have eaten more.

"Kyra, you're a good cook," I said when I had finished.

She smiled. "Thanks. I thought you'd like it. That's one of the signs." She removed the tray.

"Signs of what? Kyra, how did I get here? The last thing I knew, I was on level H."

"I brought you," she answered. She fingered her lower lip indecisively. "You might as well know, I suppose," she said. "The FBY raided H—actually it's I—and took Despoina prisoner."

"What? How did they get there?"

"I wish I hadn't told you." She pulled the pillows out from under my head and laid me back on them. "Go back to sleep," she told me. "You need more rest."

"Do you expect me to go back to sleep after you tell me a thing like that?"

"Yes," she replied sharply, "I do. I'll tell you more about it when you wake up again. Things are pretty much all right, you know."

"But Despoina—"

"They won't hurt her. Go to sleep."

Once more I slept. Kyra had turned out the light when she left, and the room was pleasantly dark. Once I heard a rustle and a scratching in the hall that half wakened me, but I soon was asleep again.

I was already awake when she came in to wash my face and, as she expressed it, service me. "I want to know what happened," I said as soon as I was cleaned up.

"Breakfast first, breakfast first," she said crossly. "I scrambled up some dehydrated eggs."

After I had eaten—the eggs were very tasty—and she had taken the dishes away, I said, "Now tell me what happened. How did the FBY get down there? When I saw the rock walls moving, just before I blacked out—was that the FBY making the raid?"

"I expect so. I don't know anything about the rock walls. But the FBY followed you down to where Despoina was."

"Followed me down? How could that be? Did you help them?"

She turned a dull, angry red. "You're the biggest fool I ever knew in my life," she said bitterly. "Help them? Of course I didn't. They tied me up and kept a gun on me. I was lucky they didn't try a little torture to make me tell."

"I beg your pardon. But how did they find the way down? I didn't leave any trail."

"Yes, you did. They have a sensing device—it's something like a manometer—that picks up the changes in pressure a human being leaves where he's been. People shed molecules into the air all the time."

"And they used that?"

"Yes. It takes them a long time to use it, though. They snuffled about on F for half a day before they finally found the autoclave."

"I don't see how they could get through the autoclave without the processing you gave me."

She grinned wryly. "One of them didn't. He made an awful mess. Going through the autoclave didn't do any of them any good. . . . Would you like to get up a while? I could make your bed."

"All right."

She put her arm under my shoulders and helped me to a sitting position on the edge of the bed. She draped a blanket around me for covering. "I haven't any robe large enough for you to get into," she said. "Hold onto my arm and I'll walk you over to the chair."

I did as she bade me. As I felt her slight body bear up firmly under my weight, I was stricken by a sort of shame. I outweighed this small girl by at least seventy pounds. And yet she had somehow got me back from level H, taken me to her own quarters, cared for all my wants, mentionable or not, for ten days.

"Kyra, you're a good girl," I said.

She turned bright pink. "Oh . . ." she said. "It's okay."

I squeezed her hand. After a moment, she returned the squeeze.

She went to work on the bed. As I watched her, I asked, "How did you get me away from the FBY?"

"I paid a price," she answered briefly.

It came to me abruptly that she was lying. I don't know why I was so sure of it. Kyra was honest, basically, but she wasn't a transparent person or especially easy to read. But I was sure she hadn't bribed the FBY to let me go. A price had been paid, certainly. But to whom?

"How much of the stuff I saw as I went through the levels was real?" I asked her.

"I don't know what you saw," she replied, tucking in the sheets.

"Well . . ." I told her what had happened on level G. "The dog, for instance. Did he really have a double brain? Or was that illusory?"

She shook her head. "I don't think so. There are . . . animals like that. I think you really did have the double sight, temporarily. Perhaps someday you'll have it for good."

"I'm not so sure I like having it. Oh, and Cindy Ann. Did she catch the plague from me?"

"I doubt it. The course of immunization the people on G have had has left them more fragile than they realize. I think she died of a heart attack."

"Kyra, are you a doctor?"

She laughed. "Of a sort. You'd better get back to bed now."

She helped me over to the bed. I lay back with a sigh of fatigue. The clean, cool sheets felt good.

"There're a lot more questions I want to ask you," I said.

"I know. But you'd better have a nap now."

When she came in with lunch, I asked her, "What's the noise I keep hearing in the hall? A rustling and scratching? I don't think it's the white rats that were in the hall before."

I thought she turned pale. She went to the hall door and tried the fastenings. "It's all right," she said, with a sigh of relief. "As long as the door's locked. . . ."

"But what was it?"

"One of the workers here—Sorensen, I think his name is—has been doing some breeding experiments with lab animals. This one can eat its way through the wire mesh of a cage as if it were tissue paper. But for some reason it never attacks wood."

"Is it carnivorous?"

"Not primarily. It loves to gnaw. But it doesn't eat what it gnaws."

I blinked. "Oh, it's not really dangerous," she said impatiently. "Wood repels it. And the door is locked."

"Is that why you were carrying the knife when I first saw you? To protect yourself?"

"One of the reasons. Level F is not without its dangers. I do have to protect myself."

"Why do you stay here, then?"

She was silent. "Eat your lunch," she said at last. "I'm running out of things to cook. I'll have to visit the stockpiles pretty soon."

As she was clearing away the tray, I said, "Sit down and talk a while. There are a lot more questions I want to ask."

"Umm," Kyra replied, but she put the tray down on a table and sat down by my bed.

"How much of my perceptions on level H were actual? What made me so sick? And why did Despoina want me to come to her? I suppose she was real, anyway."

Kyra laughed. I could smell the faint rose of the perfume she used. "Yes, Despoina was real. . . . Tell me what happened on level H. And on I, the hidden nadir level, too."

It took me quite a time. "Well," she said when I had finished, "the man in the cowl wasn't real. And the flames you saw were an illusion, too. Or, more accurately, an old memory. And it was memory that told you the proper responses to make."

"Memory? Nothing like that has ever happened to me."

She gave me an oblique look. "I didn't say *when* it had happened. But it was a memory.

"The man in the stag's mask was really there, I think," she continued. "You see, a scourging is part of the rite. The rite was interrupted by the FBY, or you would have learned the reason for it."

"And Despoina? And the men in the lions' masks?"

"They were both really there. Despoina has made some changes.... That is what makes her a great ..."

"A great what?" I asked impatiently. "Kyra, you people—you all seem to be related, somehow. You hint and hint. Ames did. Why don't you ever say anything directly? Why all the mystery?"

She laughed. "We hint partly because some things can only be said indirectly, and partly because we are not sure how much you already know. From all our hinting, you will some day, perhaps, realize that you have learned what was already there."

I sighed with exasperation and rolled my head on the pillow. Kyra laughed again. "Any more questions?"

"Yes. Why have I been so sick? Why did Despoina summon me to her?"

"You had Despoina's ring. Did you ever look at the inside of it?"

"I don't think so. The outside was what interested me."

"Yes. If you had looked at the inside, I think you would have found a thin brownish film smeared over it."

"A film of what?"

"Of certain strain of plague spores. You see, I cannot be quite certain what Despoina was trying to do. I don't know everything that was in her mind. But haven't you noticed something? You have been in my company for hours now. Do you feel any desire to get away from me?"

"No. No, I don't. That's odd."

"Not odd. It's what she was trying to do. Your infection with this particular strain, and recovery from it, have had the effect of making you able to tolerate the proximity of human beings in the way that was usual before the plagues broke out.

"Despoina infected you deliberately. Ames, who hadn't quite your—constitution, died when he put on the ring. But she has also been trying to find a simpler way of making people able to endure each other, and that is why the FBY, as an organization, has been interested in her."

"The people on level G seemed to be able to stand each other's society," I said thoughtfully. "They did it with euph pills."

Kyra shrugged. "They have to take bigger and bigger doses. After a while, they lock themselves in closets and shiver, or start banging their heads against walls."

"Cindy Ann didn't mention the head-banging."

"I imagine she was ashamed of it. It isn't the sort of thing that ought to happen to VIP's."

"But why did Despoina make me go down to her? I could have been infected by the ring, and stayed on level E. I could just as well have gone through my whole illness there."

"I told you, I don't know all that was in her mind. She doesn't confide in *me*. But I think she was testing you to make sure you are one of the old sort."

"Of the old sort? What do you mean by that?"

She shrugged. "You've already had lots of hints."

"Umm. Did I pass the test?"

"I think so. Even the difficulties you had, the places you failed, were the places where one of the old sort would fail."

I still didn't understand. Looking back on it, I think I must have been deliberately blind. "But the FBY captured her?" I asked. "Didn't she foresee that they might follow me down?"

Kyra's eyes flickered. "I keep telling you, I don't know what was in her mind. But they captured her, yes. Her, and all the people with her. The FBY has them now."

Kyra's voice hadn't changed at all, and yet I was perfectly convinced that she was lying. I couldn't believe that the woman I had seen in the twinkling light of the candles, bare-breasted and beautiful, had fallen ignominiously into the hands of the FBY.

"I wonder . . ." I said thoughtfully.

"Wonder what?" Kyra snapped the words.

"I wonder if there are any of her people still on level H."

"Well, there might be. But we'll never know."

"Why not?"

"Because the FBY, when they came up with her, sealed off the lower levels for good. Nobody can get down there again."

I said nothing. But I was resolved, as soon as I recovered my usual strength, to try to get down to level H once more.

12

THE JAILER cast the hempen rope around my throat. I knew better than to resist him; he was my friend, and this was clearly for the best.

"It will be short," he said into my ear. He put a billet of wood in the slack of the noose and began to twist. The rope bit in. I couldn't breathe any longer. My chest strove desperately. No air got past the rope. My eyes were starting from my head.

How long it took! Why didn't he hurry? Against my will my hands went up and began to fight the rope.

"Stop it," he hissed. "Better this than burning."

I bucked and labored. He held on. His kind hands inexorably tightened the rope.

I woke with a strangled cry. In the darkness I reached out for Kyra. When I had begun to have the nightmares—which she had explained as indicating that I was "developing"—she had moved her bed in beside mine, saying that if I woke without her near me, I might grow to be afraid to go to sleep.

I found her hand and pressed it. She sighed, fidgeted, and then said sleepily, "What is it, Sam?"

"I had another dream."

"Which one?"

"I dreamed I was in a jail, a dank filthy place, and the jailer was trying to strangle me—with a rope he twisted with a piece of wood. I wasn't supposed to fight him, though. I thought he was my friend."

"He probably was," she answered. She yawned and sniffled. "If you have any more dreams, Sam, I don't think you need to wake me. You can do without me now. You're getting better when you have that dream. Go back to sleep."

I gave her hand a final squeeze and rolled away from her in my bed. The last thing I thought before I fell asleep again was: She says I'm getting better. All right. Tomorrow, if I get a chance, I'll try to get through to level H.

Breakfast was instant coffee and a Danish pastry we both liked that came in cans. She was picking up the cups to take them over to the sink to wash them when I said, "Do you hear that noise in the hall? That sort of rustle and flutter? Is it what I think it is?"

She stopped, frozen, and listened. "Oh, yes, it is." She sighed. "Sorensen's home-grown monster. It'll go away again pretty soon, I suppose. I wish it would stop coming here. Most of the things on level F don't bother me, but I hate that blob of muck."

"What does it look like?"

"Never mind what it looks like. If I told you, it would just give you more material for nightmares." She went over to the sink with the cups and started rinsing them.

"Kyra, why do you stay on this level?" I asked when she came back.

"I've been stationed here," she answered briefly.

"To do something? Is that what you mean?"

"Partly that. And partly because I—"

"Because you what?"

"None of your business," she snapped. "If it's right for you to know, you'll be told."

"When I was on level F before, you made me promise to help you get back to the surface again."

"Yes."

"What did you think I could do?"

"I thought you might use your influence at court to help me get back."

"With Despoina?"

"I suppose so."

The interchange was beginning to have the maddening quality that most of my attempts to get information from Kyra ended in. I said, "What about it now? Does the promise still hold?"

"If you're able to keep it, it does. But Despoina's gone. There's nobody for you to use influence with."

She went over to a cupboard and opened it. "Nothing for lunch but dehydrated eggs," she said. "I'll have to visit the stockpiles. Do you think you can get your bath by yourself?"

This was a reference to the little shower she had rigged up in the corner of the next room. We were able to get by with living on level F because most of the labs had sinks and hot plates, with a toilet to every three or four rooms. But it lent an amateurish, camping-out quality to our domestic arrangements.

"Sure, I'll be all right. But what about Sorensen's pet? It's probably still in the hall."

"It won't bother me," she said, "as long as I have this." She picked up the knife that was so often in her hand.

"I should think a chunk of wood might be more helpful."

"No. It can't stand the noise when I make the knife twang."

I must still have looked doubtful, for she said reassuringly, "It's all right, Sam. I wouldn't go if I thought it was dangerous. I won't be gone more than half an hour."

She went to the cupboard and got out a strong cloth shopping bag. With it in one hand and the athame in the other, she walked to the door. "I'll be back soon," she said reassuringly, and went out.

I heard her footsteps receding in the hall. As soon as I felt she was safely out of the way, I got to my feet. I was still weak and wobbly; I had to stop and lean against the wall. A few steps at a time, stopping to rest and support myself on pieces of furniture, I made my way to the intercommunicating door.

The next room had been Kyra's bedroom. Now there was nothing in it but the rigged-up shower and a few changes of clothing hanging on hooks on the wall. I made my way through it and into the next room in line, which was Kyra's "consulting room." It kept being borne in on me how weak I still was.

The consulting room was just as it had been when I first saw it: it held the padded couch, the armchair with the straps, and the autoclave. The autoclave was what interested me.

I wobbled over to it. I had resolved to try to get through to level H today, and I still meant to, weak as I was. But it occurred to me that I was behaving in a somewhat disingenuous manner toward Kyra. After all, she had saved my life.

I looked around me. Under the padded couch there was a sort of sled, quite large but amateurish-looking, with a rope tied to it. I wondered if that was how Kyra had got me back from the bottom level. Well, I could reconnoiter anyway.

I opened the autoclave—the thing was as big as a bathtub—and stuck my head and shoulders inside. I reached forward and began tapping against the metal surface opposite me. It seemed perfectly solid. In my mind was a faint hope that I would touch a spring, or something of that sort, and be carried forward and into the chute without the guilt of having deliberately deserted Kyra.

That was not what happened at all. I tapped and listened for quite a long time, without getting anything more than the thin, tinny noise one would expect. Annoyed, I began to tap louder. And suddenly—I must have jarred the hinges —the lid of the autoclave came down with a clunk over my head.

I began to back out, wriggling. My shirt caught on the catch, and then on a series of projections along the bottom valve. I tried to get my arms out to help myself, but there wasn't room. Ripping loose by main force didn't work either. The shirt was cloth, not paper, and it held. I felt like a man trapped by a gigantic clam.

I tried to push up on the lid. But I was still weak from my illness, and I couldn't get any leverage. I was still in this ridiculous and embarrassing position when Kyra came in.

She could move very quietly when she chose, and the first indication I had of her presence came when she said acidly, "What are you trying to do, Sam? Steam-clean yourself?"

"Get me out," I said in muffled tones.

"No." There was a series of sounds that might have meant she was sitting down on the couch. "Not until you tell me what you were trying to do."

"I should think it would be obvious," I said with what dignity I could muster. "To get through to level H, of course."

"Level H?" She sounded really surprised. "But I told you it had been closed off. Nobody can get through to it. Didn't you believe I was telling the truth?"

"Get me out!"

"Okay." She came over to the autoclave and began tugging at my shirt. Nobody could have accused her of undue gentleness—later I found a whole series of abrasions along my spine—and when she had got me loose she gave me a slap on the buttocks that caught me off balance and almost sent me sprawling.

I turned to face her, furious. But she gave me glare for glare, her dark eyebrows knitted angrily, and after a moment I began to laugh. There was something irresistibly comic in this small girl's self-confident dignity.

"It's no laughing matter," she said severely. "I don't like being suspected of lying." She sat down on the couch.

"I'm sorry, Kyra. But—"

"But you just didn't believe me, eh?" She tossed the athame up in the air and caught it expertly.

"I'm sorry, Kyra," I said again.

She put the athame down and folded her hands in her lap. "When the FBY came up from H, they blew up G with hand grenades. G is one big rubble heap. The whole space is filled with broken masonry and pieces of twisted steel. You never saw such a mess."

It was impossible to doubt her. "What happened to the people?" I asked.

"They were all killed."

"Didn't the FBY care about killing them?"

"No, why should they? They weren't any good."

"They were all VIP's."

She shrugged. "The FBY is the new VIP's."

"Was *everybody* killed?" I asked. I was thinking of the dark-skinned woman I had shown Despoina's ring to.

Kyra looked away. "Two people got out, I think. And a dog. But nobody could get down there now unless he had a steam shovel."

"Nobody could get down there," I repeated thoughtfully.

"Oh, *somebody* might be able to. But the FBY is efficient, and they were trying to block H off. You or I couldn't get through. You'll just have to accept it, Sam.

"And now that you're so much better," she said practically, "it's time to start training and strengthening you. Have you had your bath?"

"No. What difference does it make?"

"It does, though. Have a good bath, with plenty of soap, and put on all fresh things. I'll get you a towel."

When I came back from my shower, she was waiting for me in the room with the autoclave. I had been thinking while I was getting dressed, and I tackled Kyra immediately.

"Kyra," I said, "are you Despoina in disguise?"

Her mouth came open a little. She gave me an astonished look. "Am I—what?"

"Are you Despoina? You could be, you know."

"No, I couldn't. What makes you think I could?"

"You're just about the same height—"

"No, we're not. She's several inches taller than I—"

"And you both have that very pale, pearly skin. Your hair could be dyed."

"Well, it isn't. And what about the color of our eyes?"

"I didn't get to see what color her eyes were. Your figures seem to be alike."

"No. Her breasts are larger than mine."

I wasn't satisfied, even after all these denials. "Are you a relative of hers, then? You do seem like her, somehow."

"She's an eighteenth cousin of mine, or something. A lot of people in the craft are related by blood. Sometimes it's pretty remote. . . . Now sit down in the chair. And then I'll blindfold you."

I obeyed. As she tied a square of black silk over my eyes, I realized how disappointed I was. I'd wanted Kyra to be Despoina, even though I realized, when I thought about it, that she was too short to be the woman I had seen among the columns at the bottom of H. But the communication between Despoina and me had been rudely, almost painfully, interrupted when the FBY had burst in, and I would be unsatisfied until it could be renewed once more.

I heard the spurt of a match. Kyra was holding something under my nose. "Inhale," she said, "and hold your breath until it gets uncomfortable. This will all be rather pleasant, Sam. You needn't wince."

I drew smoke into my lungs. It smelled a little like resin and a little like camphor, and quite a lot like violets. "What was that?" I asked when I had exhaled.

"We call it kat. We used to use it a good deal. But it's hard to get now, when nothing grows normally."

"I hear a noise in the hall," I said after a moment. My heartbeat had speeded up.

"Pay no attention to it," Kyra replied absently. "It's the white rats, on their usual schedule. You can hear them more plainly from this room, that's all.

"Now, draw your sight in behind your eyeballs, and look out over the top of your head. Don't try to *see* anything, particularly—just look."

I attempted to follow these impossible instructions. "I don't see anything," I said after a minute. "I don't see how I could."

"Don't you? Maybe this will help." She put her thumbs just above my eyes, in the space between the eyeball and the bony arch, and pressed lightly. "Do you see anything now?"

"Yes." I was very much excited. "I see—I see your hands, pressing. They're a dull red. And there's a sort of streamer of light coming out from them."

"Good!" She sounded pleased. "Look at me now, over the top of your head. Do you see anything?"

"Yes." I was still excited. "I see you, in a dim red outline, and there's a bright, bright spot between your eyes. There's a larger spot, not quite so bright, just under your breasts."

"That's pretty good, for the first time," Kyra said. She removed the blindfold. "We don't want you to get overtired. Now we'll try something else."

She covered one of the enameled instrument trays with several layers of paper toweling. She drew a fistful of something from a small cloth bag.

"When I ask you how many beads there are," she said, "answer right away. Don't try to count." She dropped some translucent turquoise beads on the surface of the tray, and held it out to me. "Now. How many beads are there? Don't count."

This was easy. "Four," I said.

She opened her fist and dropped more beads. "Now?"

"Uh—seven."

"Don't count," she said severely. "I told you not to. Now?"

"I can't—"

"Yes, you can. How many beads are there?"

"Thirty-six."

"And now?" She added more beads to those in the tray each time she spoke.

"Seventy-eight."

"And now?"

"I can't possibly—"

"Tell me," she said between her teeth.

"A hundred and thirteen. No, fourteen."

"That's fine. And now?" She scooped up beads from the paper toweling.

"Eighty-two."

"This time?"

"Exactly forty."

"And now?"

"You've taken them all except one. But somehow, it looks as if there were more."

"Umm." She put the beads back in the bag and put the bag in a drawer. "That's enough for now. I'll start getting us some lunch."

After we had eaten, Kyra suggested that I lie down on my bed and rest. "I'll be gone for a while," she said.

"Where do you go, Kyra? Every day, or almost every day, you go away about this time."

"I have affairs to attend to," she replied impassively. "If you can sleep for a while, do. It would do you good." She picked up the athame. "I'm not going far."

Left alone, I was restless. I tossed about for a while on the bed, and then fell into an unquiet doze. I was awakened by a knock on the door.

It startled me. Almost before I could lift my sleep-confused head from the pillow, the door opened and a man stuck his head and shoulders inside.

"Excuse me," he said when he saw me. "Is Tanith here?"

"No one's here except myself," I answered.

"Oh." He shut the door.

When Kyra returned, a little later, I told her about the caller. "He asked for Tanith," I finished.

"Tanith?" Her eyebrows went up. "What did he look like?"

"Fattish. Middle-aged. I didn't get much of a look at him. But I think I'd seen him before."

"Ah. There are all sorts of people on this level. Some of them have odd sorts of reasons for being here."

The matter seemed to be closed. But I noticed that she seemed absent and distracted the rest of the "day." (I put the word in quotation marks because, of course, there was no alternation of light and darkness on any of the tiers. But it was dark inside our sleeping room when Kyra turned the light out; we stayed awake for sixteen hours or so, and then slept for about eight.)

We went to bed early, since I was tired. I woke once in the night to hear the peculiar rustle and scratching that meant Sorensen's production was outside our door. But the door was locked, and I heard Kyra breathing quietly in her bed beside me. We were safe, Kyra and I, from whatever dangers prowled the corridors of level F.

Next day Kyra went on with my training and strengthening. There was a series of games—plays—seemingly childish and meaningless, that yet felt important and significant.

For example, once she had me blindfold myself and then edge my way cautiously around the walls of the room, telling me that I was walking a narrow path high on a mountain cliff.

Abruptly she told me to stop. I obeyed, halting in mid-step. "What would have happened if I hadn't stopped?" I asked her when she had taken the blindfold off.

"There was a gap in the path. You would have fallen and been killed."

I thought she must be joking, but when I looked at her, her face was perfectly serious.

We repeated the training gambits of the day before, too. But as soon as we had finished lunch, Kyra had me try something different.

She gave me a white pill to swallow, explaining that it was a mild anesthetic. "It's not a hypnotic, or even a sedative," she said. "I'm not trying to make you go to sleep, but to dull your awareness of sense impressions. Now, lie down on your bed."

When I was lying flat, she put a black mask over my eyes. "I don't want any light at all to get through—it's not just that I'm trying to keep you from seeing things," she said.

"What's the idea of all this?" I asked.

"By cutting out all avenues of sense reception, I want to throw you back on yourself. Try not to move about restlessly. Just lie still and let your thoughts come."

"What if I go to sleep?" I asked.

"I don't think you will, but if you do, it's all right. I'll be in the next room, with the door open, in case you get frightened. Is there anything else before I put the ear-stops in?"

"How long am I to stay like this?"

"Not more than five or six hours, anyway. I'll look at you from time to time and see how you're doing. Okay?"

I nodded. Gently she inserted the plugs in my ears.

Now, being blind and deafened, with one's sense impressions dulled, is a little like going to sleep in a quiet room. And yet it was thoroughly unlike that. Almost from the moment that Kyra put the plugs in my ears, a series of brilliant pictures began to form behind the lids of my closed eyes.

They were architectural, primarily—columned galleries, balustrades with carved members, rooms with groined ceilings and coffered walls and sides. All these in brilliant colors, the ceilings picked out in gold and red and green, the columns glowing amber against an intense blue sky.

The pictures succeeded one another rapidly. They were there a moment, and then they would be gone. Sometimes the same elements would appear in a new combination, as if a kaleidoscope had been shaken, and sometimes the picture would seem entirely new, with nothing in the one before to prepare me for it.

For a long time I watched them with absorbed interest. I was not restless, I had no desire to move my body about, and I was certainly not asleep. But as the flow of pictures continued without the slightest slowing, it became at first tiresome, then oppressive, and finally frightening.

And still it continued. There was no place for me to go to withdraw from it. Still the staircases rose, the battlements ascended, the great painted gates loomed up. At last, with a tremendous effort, I withdrew my—mind? attention? self?—from the incessant pictures, and let them form themselves. I was no longer there.

I—or somebody called Sam—was in a sad, dull, dun-colored place, a world of dim light and color, a flat, featureless plain. It was an afterworld. It never changed.

I was roused by Kyra withdrawing the plugs from my ears. "I'm going to uncover your eyes," she said into my ear, "but don't open them immediately. There. Now, how do you feel?"

I considered. "As if I'd been dead."

"And—?"

"Guilty. In dying, there is always some guilt."

"Any horror?" she asked professionally.

"Yes! Yes!"

"You may open your eyes now. How do you feel toward *me?*"
Emotion welled up in me. "I hate you," I said.

She laughed. "Well, that's only natural. Do you want to get away
from me?"

"No. I want to stay and strangle you."

Again she laughed. She sat down beside me on the bed. "You are
greatly improved," she said.

"Why did you rouse me when you did?" I asked her.

"When I looked in, just now, tears were flowing down your
cheeks."

I drew a long, wavering sigh. "How long was I cut off like that?"

"About four hours. The results would have been even better if I'd
been able to put you in a bath of water held just at body temperature.
But of course I haven't the facilities. You may get up now, Sam, but
move slowly. You'll be shaky for a while."

I sat up slowly, yawning and rubbing my face. I swung my feet
over the side of the bed and stood up. "My sense of time's confused,"
I told her. "It could be either midnight, or a new day."

"Yes. Come into my consulting room and I'll show you something
else. You will have to work hard before you can do this."

When we were in the room with the padded couch and the autoclave, she said, "I'm not going to blindfold you for this. But turn your
eyes toward the corner, away from me, until I tell you you may look."

I complied. I heard the rushing noise of the white rats in the corridor. At last, after perhaps five minutes, Kyra's voice said, "Now you
may look."

I turned toward the noise. She wasn't there.

I hadn't heard her go toward the door, I hadn't felt it open. I said,
"Where are you?"

"Right here." Her voice was perfectly clear, and it came from the
same spot where she had been standing when she had had me turn
my eyes away.

"But—I don't see you."

"Look closely."

"I—there's a sort of blur there. But I don't see you, Kyra. You're not there at all."

"That's fine. I haven't done this much recently." Suddenly she was visible, standing just where the blur had been.

"What was that?" I asked in amazement.

"Fith-fath. Shape-shifting. It's what's behind the stories about members of the craft being able to cast a sort glamour over the eyes. It is difficult to do, and exceedingly exhausting for the practitioner."

Indeed, she did look exhausted. Her forehead was beaded with sweat, and there were heavy lines of fatigue around her mouth and eyes.

"You mean you could make yourself invisible by something you did with your mind?"

"Yes. It is terribly difficult to do, and can only last a little while."

"But—how could you have any effect on my eyes?"

She shrugged. "We don't know how it works."

"Will I be able to do that?"

"I think so. If you try hard."

There was a silence. She had sunk down on the couch, her head drooping. From the hall I heard once more the noise of the white rats.

"That's odd," I said. "The rats are back ahead of schedule. It's only a little while since I heard them leaving the corridor before."

Kyra raised her head and listened. She drew in her breath.

"I don't like this," she said after a moment. "They're sensitive to vibration, you know. The last time they were badly off schedule like this was just before the FBY followed you down."

13

THE CORRIDOR was filled with a glittering, icy fog, through which, at the far end, I dimly saw the squat padded shapes of men moving. They were backing toward us, with big hoses in their hands, and the mouths of the hoses gave out drifts and billows of snow.

The fog gleamed as if the moon shone on it. Everything was perfectly silent; and it looked as if the air had begun to freeze into big soft flakes that settled slowly to the floor.

I closed the door hastily. Already I was shaking with cold. To Kyra I said, "It's the FBY. That's why the rats were off schedule yesterday. They're filling the level with CO_2 snow."

"It's not the FBY," she answered listlessly. She was leaning against the wall. "*They* think you're dead—I made them see you lying on a rock heap in G. This is the disposal people. Jaeger must have told."

"Jaeger? Who's he? But never mind that now, Kyra—we've got to get out of here."

"Where to?" she said. "There's no place we can go. G has been closed off, and they'll have guards stationed at the exits up to E."

"Aren't there any emergency exits?"

"Yes, several. But they're all in the corridor. If we go out, the disposal squad will turn the hoses on us."

"But—are we just going to stay here and be frozen to death?"

She raised her head and gave me a vague glance. "What else can we do?" she asked. "There isn't anything..."

She had been holding the athame in one hand. Now she raised it to her eyes, looked at it, and let it drop indifferently on the floor.

I stared at her unbelievingly. This lassitude, this hopeless resignation on the part of one whom I had always seen calm, optimistic, and self-assured, struck me as unnatural and inexplicable. I could hardly grasp it. I realized how much I had come to rely on her.

"There must be something we can try!" I exclaimed after a second.

"What?" Her teeth were chattering. And then, not to me, she said, "Why don't you help us? You called him to you, but I saved his life. Haven't I been punished enough? Does he have to suffer too?"

I did not know what she meant, or to whom she was speaking. Indeed, I hardly noticed her words, for an idea had come to me, seemingly from nowhere.

"Kyra, what about those yeasts and fungus spores you go to take care of in the afternoons? You've quite a large collection. Isn't there something among them that could help us now?"

She drew in her breath. "Yes," she said thoughtfully, "there's one fungus that thrives at low temperatures. It causes hallucinations that one doesn't remember afterwards. Perhaps it . . . But we can't get through to my shop. The only access is through the corridor."

She sank back again against the wall. "We can get through," I told her confidently. Her hopelessness had ceased to affect me, and I felt ready to smile. "That play with the mirror you showed me yesterday—we can use that to help ourselves."

"Yes . . . I suppose so. . . . Oh, it's cold in here." But she got the mirror with its pendant light from the cupboard, and handed it to me.

I opened the door a crack and peered out. "They're nearer," I said. "Two of them are facing our way."

I spun the mirror in its frame. The metal was so cold it hurt my hands. "Which way is your shop?" I asked. "We'll both have to go. Anybody who stays here will be frozen."

"Straight down the corridor to the first crossing, then left. After that I'll guide you."

"All right." The mirror was spinning nicely now. "I'm going to try to project something I think they'll be interested in," I told her. "When I open the door, run for it. I'll stay an instant to be sure the mirror works."

I hooked the mirror over the upper edge of the door. It was rotating well, filling the room with flashes of light. The door opened outward, I knew. I hesitated for a moment, remembering what Kyra had taught me. Then I flung the door wide.

A chilling air rushed in. Kyra, bent over, ran out past me. I saw a dazzle of light and then something floating serenely on the drifting surface of the layer of fog, like a flower.

There was no noise from the disposal people, but they had stopped dead in their tracks. I knew I had to hurry. I put all my skill into what Kyra had taught me to do.

The dazzle of light increased, and then began to jet up and break, like a fountain. Atop it, bobbing about like a ball in a stream, I "caused" a life-sized, tenanted, disposal bag.

It was time. The air was so cold that deep breathing would freeze my lungs. I bent over and ran.

They didn't turn the hoses on me. I was almost invisible in the wheel of light the mirror made, and besides, the appearance of the bag had made them nervous and hesitant. I tore down the corridor, turned left, and caught up with Kyra. The odd thing was that, except for us, nobody on level F seemed aware of the incursion of the disposal squads.

Kyra caught my hand. The air was warmer here. We were both panting, but we did not dare to slow down much.

She led me through a maze of turnings. We were running more slowly now. I had lost all sense of direction. At last she stopped by a frosted-glass door.

Kyra's shop was a big room, shadowlessly lighted, with rows of benches and glass frames stacked in tiers above them. "Some of my babies like the light," she said. "The one we're after doesn't care, one way or the other. What it needs is cold."

She got out one of the glass frames. Its sides were opaque plastic, and a thermometer clipped to it showed that the temperature within was minus 14 degrees centigrade.

"Do you smell anything?" she asked, looking up at me.

I inhaled. "I think so. A summery sort of smell, like grass and privet hedges?" She nodded.

"That's what causes the hallucinations," she said. "The fungus gives off that sweet scent as a by-product of its metabolism. Try to keep from breathing in very much of it."

"Can it get through the disposal people's protective suits?"

"I think so. It's very volatile, and there'll be a lot of it. When this little cryogen really gets started, it spreads fast. The CO_2 is just what it needs for rapid growth."

"How are you planning to use it?"

"It will walk up a gradient of cold. I think, if I scatter it in the hall, it will proliferate in the direction of the disposal squad."

She tucked the glass frame under her arm and started toward the door. Once more I had been asking questions and she had been answering them, but the relationship between us had changed.

"Kyra, what I want to do is to try to get through to F1, sideways. You're better at the sight than I am, by far. Before you go out in the hall, look and see where the squad and the guards are now."

Obediently she put the glass frame down on one of the benches. She closed her eyes and laid her hands crisscross over them. "I'm trying to find the entrance to F1," she said after a moment. "Here it is. Yes, there's a guard, a man with a hose and a gun, stationed there."

"How about the squad?"

"Either they've split up, or there are two squads. One's coming this way, though they may not turn. . . . Yes, they've turned. They're coming down this corridor, though they're a long way off. They're between us and the entrance to F1."

She took her hands down from her eyes and looked at me hopelessly. "It wasn't any use," she said. "I told you so."

There was reason for despair, but I did not feel it. "Have they got the corridor solidly blocked with the snow?"

"No. Not yet."

"Then we'll get through," I told her.

Her face was still full of doubt, but I picked up the frame with the fungus and went to the door. I opened it enough to see that the disposal people were still a good way off. Then I slipped off the cover of the frame, plunged my hand into it, and, with the motion of a man sowing grass seed, began to toss the cryogenic fungus out into the corridor.

It was very cold, and burned and stung my hands; afterwards I found frost-bitten patches on them. The fungus itself was beautiful, glittering delicate stuff, icy-white, and shaped like the frost flowers on a window pane.

It fell noiselessly from my hand and drifted gently toward the floor. For a moment nothing happened. Kyra had come to my side at the door and was peering out through the opening with me. But an icy breath blew toward us, and the pretty stuff began to respond to it.

Slowly at first, and then with growing speed, it began to spread out. The motion toward the disposal men at first was almost imperceptible. But it increased, and the cryogen thickened away from us.

Kyra was shaking with excitement. I felt her fingers digging into my arm. "If it—But there'll still be the hoses," I heard her saying.

I put my arm around her waist and held her, while the fungus, always more swiftly, grew down the corridor toward the armored men. The last few feet of its progression were like a wave racing toward a rock.

Something must have alarmed the disposal people, for all the fungus' noiselessness. Two of them spun toward us, the mouths of their hoses giving billows of white. They made warding-off motions toward what must have been an unexpected and threatening sight. But the fungus leaped at them almost joyously. The concentration of cold around the hoses was a delicacy for them; and greedily the crystalline growth clustered and clung. In no time at all the mouths of the hoses bore great choking pendant blobs of the stuff.

I don't know whether the disposal people ever caught sight of Kyra and me or not. The fungus was climbing cheerfully from the hoses up along their armor and toward the face plates of their cold-proof suits. I caught a great gush of the summer perfume—white syringa and fresh-mown grass—that the cold-loving growth gave out.

The men in the padded suits were staggering drunkenly now. One of them put his hose down carefully on a bank of fungus. He bowed politely at the man nearest him, thumbed his nose at him, and attempted an elaborate dance step. Then he collapsed face downward on a mound that was partly crystalline fungus and partly CO_2 snow.

The others reeled about in similar fashion. One of them spun dizzily like a dancing mouse; another seemed to be trying to chin himself on a non-existent horizontal bar. But at last they were all lying in abandoned attitudes on the whiteness that carpeted the corridor. The mouths of the hoses, stoppered by the fungus, had long ago ceased to eject new snow.

I turned to Kyra. "Are they unconscious?" I asked.

"No. But what they are seeing has no relation at all to the reality before their eyes."

"Then it's time for us to try to get through."

"All right." For the first time since the invasion of F had begun, Kyra seemed her old self-confident self. "Fill your lungs here, and try not to breathe as we go over the fungus. Very much of that sweet stuff, and we'll be as high as *they* are."

I hesitated. Kyra saw what was in my mind, for she said, "I don't think the cold will bother us. When my fungus grows, it warms things up."

"Fine." I took her hand and opened the door.

We had both filled our lungs. We set off at a pelting run toward the disposal squad, who by now were pretty well covered up by Kyra's fungus. As soon as we hit sizable patches of the fungus, our pace slowed; it was fluffy under our feet, and running through it was like running through soft snow.

Ahead of us there were the mounded forms of the disposal people, and then a rising slope of CO_2 snow over which the fungus grew luxuriantly. Further on, the ice hill filled the corridor completely, except for a clear space at the upper left-hand side.

Our run had slowed to not much more than a plodding walk; we had to lift our knees high at each step. I had had to breathe, and I had an exceedingly vivid picture of Ames, hanging from a rope ladder and grinning like a monkey, offering me a pair of snowshoes. In a moment I recognized it for what it was, a hallucination caused by the fungus. But it frightened me.

We clambered over the bodies of the disposal people and started up the slope of ice. It was not unbearably cold here, but the summer perfume from the fungus was almost tangible. I kept slipping into patches of hallucination, and dragging myself out of them painfully.

It was too much for me. The unreal appearances before me were no longer frightening, but welcome. I would sit down comfortably where I was and enjoy them.

Kyra, or somebody, looked at me with a desperate face. With the last of her strength she twisted my hand savagely about on my wrist. The pain cleared my head for a moment, and I realized that we were at the very top of the long ice slope.

Kyra had sunk to her knees, vanquished by the fungus she had reared. I caught her under the armpits and threw her forward over the crest and down the slope. Then—but this was really the last effort I could make—I launched myself after her.

We went bumping and skidding down the other side. We reached bottom with a thud and a crash. Here I think we lay for a considerable time. But the air that lapped our faces was cold, free of the summer intoxication of the fungus, and at last I got unsteadily to my feet.

I looked about me. To the left, the direction from which the disposal people had come, the corridor was solidly blocked with the sub-zero CO_2 snow. But the right fork lay free. And the ice barrier between us and the entrance to F1 lay behind us. We were on the other side.

14

THOUGH THE hill of ice lay behind us, between us and the entrance to F1 was the guard Kyra had seen, with a CO_2 tank on his back, and a gun. He might shoot us, or he might freeze us; it wouldn't make much difference to us which he did.

What we must do, essentially, was to get past the guard at the entrance without his knowing we had done so. We had evaded the disposal people twice by causing hallucinations—once physically, by means of the cryogen's exhalation, and once psychologically, by the mirror game. The mirror was out of reach, but could we use the cryogenic fungus again?

As if she had picked up my thoughts, Kyra said, "The ice fungus won't help us. There isn't any snow near the guard for it to grow on. Besides, we couldn't stand another exposure to it ourselves. It's cumulative. We'd be seeing visions before he did. We'll have to think of something else." She gave me a questioning, hopeful look.

I shook my head to clear it. The breath of summer still hung in the air, and I found it hard to concentrate.

The light was bright enough everywhere on level F for a luminous object to be difficult to see. But the ice hill cast a shadow; and there, in a localized patch of darkness, pale blue and glowing against the wall, I saw the sign of the double axe.

I thought it must be a hallucination. But Kyra was looking at it too, with wide eyes and parted lips. "I never saw the sign written like that before," she said slowly. "With the head down and the handle pointing up."

"Do you think—" And then, realizing what the sign meant, my words came out tumbling over each other. "Kyra, is there an emergency exit in this part of the corridor? In the ceiling?"

"Yes! Yes, there is!"

"Then that's it. Can you open it?"

"I can try."

She began running her hands along the part of the side wall nearest us, apparently aimlessly. For a few moments nothing happened. But she repeated the sliding motions several times, and at last a square section of the corridor ceiling slid away, leaving a dark opening above us. I felt a faint down-draft of air.

"Too bad we can't really fly on broomsticks," said Kyra, looking up at the hole. She was shivering violently—more from nervous tension, I thought, than from cold. "You'll have to put me up on your shoulders, Sam, and help me through. Once I'm up, there'll be a rope ladder or something I can throw down to you."

She kicked off her high-heeled shoes. I picked her up and, after a few fumbles, managed to set her feet on my shoulders. She couldn't have weighed more than ninety pounds.

She balanced unsteadily. Then, "Lift me!" she cried. Simultaneously she gave a spring upward and clutched with her hands. There must have been something for her to grasp, for in a moment I heard her panting above my head.

The end of a knotted rope tapped me on the chest. "Hurry!" Kyra said. "They're coming, only a couple of turnings off. . . . Don't forget my shoes."

I stuck the shoes in my pocket and shinned up the knotted rope. As soon as I was through the opening, Kyra pressed a button and it began to close.

I looked down. Nobody was coming in the corridor, and the ice hill glinted brilliantly under the never-changing illumination of the level. For a moment I had the fancy that a new ice age had begun, and that F was a wide plain over which extended the silent lunar triumph of the snow.

The hatch had closed. We were standing in a space about four feet square, with a narrow chute reaching upwards directly over our heads. It was not completely dark; the walls and chute had a phosphorescent covering, and we could see each other's face dimly.

Kyra laid her finger warningly to her lips and pointed to the chute. Once more I boosted her up—it was easier this time—and she let down another rope for me, which I went up. I gave her her shoes, and we began to climb.

The chute was like a narrow chimney, with hand and foot holds cut at convenient intervals. We were only a few feet up when I heard a vague, confused noise from the corridor below and realized that the disposal squad must be there. Now I knew why Kyra had laid her finger to her lips.

We climbed steadily. I could not believe that we had escaped the disposal people so easily, but as the moments passed without pursuit and our immunity became more and more evident, I was dizzy with relief. I had a winy sense of being a favorite of fate.

Still we climbed. It seemed to me that nothing in my past, not even the descent to Despoina, had prepared me for this. Then I had wandered through a phantasmagoria of past lives. Now I was climbing toward a future whose shape I could not even picture to myself.

Kyra had stopped now and again to rest, leaning against the side of the chute and breathing hard. It was after one of these halts that she said softly, "It's all right to talk now, Sam."

My high-flown, amorphous speculations dropped away from me abruptly. "Is this supposed to be an emergency *exit?*" I said in a whisper. "We've climbed far enough to get to E twice over. And in a real emergency, nobody would have been able to get into it at all."

Kyra chuckled softly. "The levels are full of foul-ups and bright ideas that didn't work. They had so much money to spend when they were enlarging the caves and laying out the levels that they made plenty of mistakes. But it does get up to E eventually."

More climbing. The sides of the chute had roughened and grown darker. At last Kyra said, "I think this is about it."

"E, you mean?"

"No, not yet. But there ought to be a place about here where we can rest."

She halted and leaned against the right side of the chimney. Looking up, I saw her push hard against the surface to her left. Nothing happened. She waited a moment, braced herself, and shoved again.

This time it worked. The whole left-hand side of the chute cracked outward, away from her hands, with a dull snap. Through the irregular opening, the phosphorescent walls of a room were dimly visible.

"What was that?" I asked. The wall had broken like a slab of peanut candy.

"A lichen. It looks just like the rest of the chute, and it's pretty strong. But if one knows just where to push, it breaks. There was a lot of use made of fungi and lichens just before the plagues began.

"Let's go in. I'm tired. There's no reason why we shouldn't rest."

I followed her into a room that reminded me of the attics I had played in in Peabody when I was a boy. It was large, with an unpainted wooden floor, and the only furniture was a wide bunk and a chemical toilet discreetly visible behind a screen.

"Why was this built?" I asked, looking around.

Kyra shrugged. "I imagine the designer had some sort of notion of guerilla fighters resting here between sallies out to harass the enemy after they had taken level F. But I really don't know. Perhaps he was only trying to bolster up the economy by spending a little more cash.

"Let's sit down. No wonder I'm tired. We only had a few hours' sleep, and ever since the disposal people came, we've been running, or climbing, or afraid. There's something very tiring about being afraid."

She sat down on the bunk and, after a moment drew her feet up and stretched out on it. I sat down beside her.

"Are we safe here?" I asked.

"I think so. When I'm tired I only have the sight in patches. But as far as I can see, the disposal people are still at work in the corridors. The ones we gassed are slowly coming to. They don't think that anybody escaped, you see."

I pondered. "Didn't the game with the mirror make them suspicious?"

"Not any more than they were before. F has always had the reputation of being an odd place, where uncanny and 'scientific' things happen."

"It's odd nobody else on F tried to get away," I said. "The cold woke us both. But nobody else seems to have noticed it."

"I suppose the disposal people put a hypnotic in the air supply before they came down. It didn't affect us because we're not quite the same as most people, physically. Or there might be some other reason."

It was very quiet in the bare, lofty room. When Kyra stopped talking, I could hear the beating of my own heart. The quiet made me realize how constant the background of noise in F had been. Some of it had been meaningless, some of it had been threatening. But it had always been there.

"You said Jaeger must have told. Who's he?"

"He's the man who asked you about Tanith the other day. He goes around asking for her," Kyra replied. "He's one of the few people who got out of one of those plastic disposal bags."

I thought of the slowly moving dead man I had seen when I had been helping with the bulldozing. "Got out of it? You mean he wasn't dead when they put him in?"

"Yes. Or so he says. Myself, I think he saw them burying Tanith, his girl. Anyhow, it left him with a *thing* about people he doesn't know. He's apt to think they're plague vectors. I stopped him from putting in an anonymous call to the disposal people once before."

"Would they freeze off a whole level just on the strength of an anonymous call?" I asked.

"I don't know what he told them," Kyra said. She yawned. "If you're done asking questions, Sam, why don't you lie down too? A nap would do us both good. And then we can go on up to E."

"Just one more question. Why were you so hopeless when we first knew the disposal people had come?"

"It reminded—None of your business, Sam. Lie down. Go to sleep."

I obeyed the first command, but I could not go to sleep. My mind was too full of questions and uncertainties. At last, after I had lain beside her for a long time, I said in a whisper, "Kyra, are you asleep?"

"Not yet."

"What will you do when you get up to E?"

"Stay there a few days, until F thaws out again. Then I'll go back down. I've been stationed there.

"You can stay above ground, Sam. You'll be all right. I've done all I can for you."

Once more there was silence. The prospect she had outlined for me filled me with an odd dismay. The future without Kyra—what sort of a future would it be? And now I knew what this small girl meant in my life. She had returned the future to me as an object of speculation, even of hope. She had given my future back to me.

I rolled toward her and took her in my arms. "Kyra," I said, "let me go back with you when you go. Let me stay on F with you. If you have to stay there, I'll stay. We're close to each other already, darling. Already we're half in love. We could be happy together, even on F. It's an unpleasant place, but we'd be lovers, dear."

She had not resisted my embrace, but she had not yielded to it. "No," she said softly. "I'm sorry, Sam."

I did not let her go. "Why not?" I said. "Don't you feel close to me, too?"

"Oh, yes. But there's a reason why we can't be lovers, Sam."

"What is it? Some sort of prohibition, like the one that makes you stay on F?"

"No, not that. . . . I'll have to tell you. I'm your sister, Sam."

I let her go, and she rolled out of my arms. I half sat up, leaning on one elbow, and looked down at her. She looked up at me unwinkingly.

"My sister? Are you sure? How long have you known?"

"Yes, I'm sure. I've known since you first told me your name."

I sat up on the edge of the bunk, my head between my hands. Her tone had brought conviction to me. There would be explanations; she would tell me how this extraordinary thing could be possible.

I did not doubt she had told me the truth. But now my future opened out blankly ahead of me.

15

I PARTED from Kyra, sadly and a little flatly, two days later on level E. In that interval we had done a lot of talking. She had told me the details of her begetting, as far as she knew them: she was certainly, if not my sister, my half-sister. My father—she knew his first name—had been sympathetic to the craft. Kyra's mother, who had been of high enough rank to wear the ritual bracelet, had met him one May eve, and, as Kyra put it, "taken quite a shine" to him. May eve is one of the eight ritual occasions, and Kyra herself had been the not-unanticipated result.

I hadn't known my father was interested in the old worship, but it was perfectly possible; he had been killed in a freeway wreck while I was still a baby, and I had had no opportunity to learn what he was like. I tried to find out from Kyra whether the episode had antedated or postdated my parents' marriage, but she was vague about the dates. She wasn't, it seemed, quite certain how old she was. But she had been told her father's name, and had always called herself Kyra Sewell.

"Will F be thawed out now?" I asked as we stood at the head of the stairs in our leave-taking.

"I think so. The disposal people will have cleaned up things by now. Sorensen's monster ought to have been put out of business, that's one comfort. But it's going to be odd down there, with nobody on the level but myself."

"Do you have to go back, Kyra?" I asked. I disliked thinking of her, alone and essentially defenceless, in that enormous uncanny place.

"Yes. I told you, I've been stationed here. Besides, I want to see if any of the fungi in my shop are still alive. But"—she gave me a quick smile—"I may not have to stay there much longer.

"Good-bye." She leaned forward and kissed me on both cheeks, like a pre-plague French general pinning a medal on somebody. She pressed my left hand. Then she turned and started down the stair to F.

I watched her dark head descending until she was out of sight. Small, brave Kyra! I was proud to be related to her.

I looked about me. Was I going to set up housekeeping again on one of the upper levels, or should I look about for a place to live outside? There would be plenty of vacancies above ground—the housing shortage has been solved in a way that Karl Marx, writing away in London on tracts and working for the revolution, would never have dreamed of. But it is rare to find a house or apartment where the water runs; and electric power, except near the FBY's offices, has been off for years. Nobody keeps the generators running, you see.

It would be more comfortable, certainly, to find another pad somewhere in the upper levels, but I decided I didn't want any part of it. I was sick of the artificial, microcosmic world of the caves. It would be worth putting up with inconveniencies to have sunlight and air.

I took the escalators up to the surface. It was a bright day, and I blinked like a mole as the light hit my eyes. The levels are well lighted, but the light isn't the same as up above. Then I set out on my househunting.

I found an apartment easily, on the second floor of a building that had been new when the plagues began. I thought the second floor would be a good choice because, if the roof leaked, there would be a couple of stories between me and the rain. I believe somebody was living on the ground floor, even though most of the windows were broken.

My new domain was roomy, and far enough from where the bodies are being buried to be fairly quiet. But it was unspeakably dirty. The caves are clean, partly because the air supply is filtered and partly because of the robot cleaners. But here there was a ten-years' accumulation of dust. It was so heavy and thick that it blurred the outlines of chairs and tables. It was like the furry scum that veils rocks at the bottom of a lake. But I was glad to be above ground again.

I went to the supply closet to look for a duster. There was a vacuum cleaner there, and on impulse I plugged it in and pressed the switch. To my intense surprise, the machine began to hum obediently.

The power was on. Somebody must be tending the generators again. But why? And who?

There were a few cans in the cupboard, and I dined on chow mein and applesauce. I was used to better catering. Tomorrow or the next day I would visit the stockpiles and bring back some food.

I went to bed early. Somehow, even though the power was on again, I was unwilling to turn on the lights and make known my presence.

Next morning I walked over to where the bulldozers were working and climbed up to my seat on my old machine. Nobody seemed to have noticed my absence at all.

At noon I asked Jim, the one fellow worker whose name I knew, whether he thought a man could have been put in a plastic disposal bag before he was dead and then have escaped from it. He answered that it was *possible,* but he thought it was mighty god-damned unlikely. When they were dead, they were dead.

It was odd to observe how, while we were talking, he kept backing away from me, when I moved toward him. I could approach him without discomfort, but he wanted to get away from me. I don't know whether he noticed it or not.

The day went on, with me in the peaceful frame of mind I had experienced before when bulldozing. About mid-afternoon two FBY men went by, conspicuous in their neat plum-colored uniforms. They were walking side by side, closer than most people would have done. I had seen a lot of FBY men today—one by himself as I walked to work; three going past the bulldozers in the morning; and now these two going in the other direction. Usually they kept off the streets.

On my way home from work, I made a detour to one of the stockpiles and picked up a couple of shopping bags full of delicatessen food. I knew the locations of at least eight stockpiles. Two of them were not in the levels system at all. The contents of the various stockpiles are quite individual—some run to one type of foodstuff and some to another—and the smallest of them would feed the city's present population for more than a hundred years.

I ate my evening meal and went to bed early again. Before I fell asleep I felt an acute throb of longing for Kyra. Was she safe? F was an uncanny place. I wished we had agreed on some way to communicate with each other. But she had said she might not have to stay there much longer.

My life began to settle into a routine. Daytimes I worked with the bulldozer (Jim tried to impress me into the night squad, but I turned him down), and in the evenings I read until it got dark and then went to bed. I still felt reluctant to turn on the lights in my apartment, and this forced an early bedtime. I thought of Kyra a good deal at first, and then less and less frequently. The future had ceased to occupy my mind at all.

On the surface, it seemed that nothing had changed from what it had been before I had gone down so deep, hunting Despoina. And yet I was aware that much in myself was changing, and had changed. It was a time of preparation and silent growth.

The first open change, though, came in the world about me. I had been above ground for a little more than two weeks when, going to my favorite stockpile for food on my way home from work, I found an armed man standing guard there. The shelves had been closed off by a metal gate.

The fluors lit up his face. He wore a purple uniform, of a cut identical to those worn by the FBY men, but several shades darker in color, and his face was not an FBY face. It lacked the easy affability that was almost their trademark. And yet there was a thoroughly FBY look to him. As Kyra would have said, "It stuck out all over the place."

"Stop where you are," he said sharply when he saw me. He had a rather high voice. "What do you want?"

"I came for some food," I answered. I indicated my brace of shopping bags.

"Go register at the post office. They'll give you a food card." He grinned at me unpleasantly. "From now on you lazy bums are going to have to work."

I was silent for a moment. Should I tell him I *was* working? Certainly my exertions with the bulldozer could be considered work. But I didn't think it was any of his business. Besides, I only worked for diversion and to keep from having to think.

"What are we to work at?" I asked finally. "Nobody needs to work at making things. There's enough in the piles to last for generations. And how can we work at regular jobs, when we can't stand getting near each other?"

"We'll fix that," he answered. "You'll stand it when you get hungry enough."

He had spoken with great decision. But he involuntarily gave ground when I advanced a step toward him.

"Who told you to stand guard there?" I asked him.

"The government."

"What government?"

"The new government."

Once more I moved toward him, and once more he backed away.

"Get back," he said sharply. I took another step toward him. The bullet hit the ground at my feet.

"That's a warning," he said viciously. "Get on over to the post office. I'll shoot higher next time."

I turned with what dignity I could muster and walked away with my empty shopping bags.

As I plodded along I was thoughtful. The "new government" could only be the FBY, which had for a long time been the nearest thing to a government we had. Now it seemed to be reaching for overt power.

Our society had ceased to exist because the ancient whip, hunger, could not be plied in the presence of abundance, and the ancient cement, love, could no longer operate. But if an artificial scarcity could be produced, hunger might drive us to endure each other again. We might loathe, and yet tolerate. And then we should once more live in a society.

The FBY's motives, of course, were thoroughly impure. They were not aiming at our benefit, but at their own dominance. And, since power is an appetite that grows with eating, they would soon want more.

Well, it might not be too bad. It would probably take a considerable time, four or five years, before they began to arrogate the privileges of an elite to themselves openly. And they might never become overtly cruel.

Certainly I disliked the idea. There was something painfully anti-climactic in reflecting that all the sufferings of the plague years, the deaths of nine-tenths of the population, our frozen isolation from each other—that all these miseries had served merely to put a watered-down version of a police state in power. But there wasn't much I could do about it. They had the guns.

I had been walking along slowly, while my shopping bags flapped windily around my knees. Now I realized that I was still hungry. My interview with the guard hadn't filled my belly. What should I do, go to the post office to register?

No, I wasn't hungry enough for that yet. It would be a long time before I was. I'd try at another stockpile.

The one I decided to try was really a stockpile of clerical supplies, with the foodstuffs added more or less as an afterthought, and for that very reason I thought the "new government" might have neglected to post a guard there. Cans of multi-purpose food, no matter how abundant, are not attractive except to a really hungry man.

This pile was in a big warehouse, not far from the one where I had once moved boxes. It was a tedious walk. But when I got there and went inside an armed man was standing guard.

He had the same high voice, the same tight face (did the FBY turn them out of a mold?), and the same purple uniform. And I had the same humiliating conversation with him I had had with the other guard.

I had turned away and was about to leave, angry but impotent, when the outer warehouse door opened and a man came waddling in.

His face was streaked with red and yellow paint, and he hopped like a duck. He wore a tattered crimson shirt and faded ocher trousers. In one hand he held a large stoppered Ehrenmeyer flask.

He advanced toward us, singing. "Pillicock sat on pillicock hill, Halloo, halloo, loo, loo!" He stopped and licked his lips. "This cold night will turn us all to fools and madmen," he said confidentially. He picked his nose.

Both the guard and I had backed away from him, in our minds the same thought—that this Shakespearean lunatic was a Sower, and the flask in his hand held the seeds of plague.

The guard said, "Go away, go to the post office," in a trembling voice. He half-raised his gun, and then put it down again. He knew that if he shot the man, the flask in his hand might break.

"Avaunt, you curs!" said the man in the crimson shirt. "I do not like the fashion of your garments." He grinned wolfishly and shook the flask at us.

I was frightened; in this moment I hardly remembered that I might be immune to plague. But the guard was terrified. As the man moved forward, singing something about pelican daughters, he stood for a moment trembling, and then turned and ran. His gun fell unheeded on the warehouse floor.

He got to the door, fumbled with the knob, and threw the door open. I heard the receding thud of his feet.

"Hey the doxy over the dale," said the painted man in a normal voice. He pulled a handkerchief from his hip pocket and started wiping his face. The red and yellow streaks came off easily, like grease paint. Now that he had straightened up, I saw that he was considerably taller than I had first thought.

"That's one way of getting rid of them," he said, nodding toward the open door. "The FBY people are all scared to death of Sowers and wild yeasts. Unfortunately, it isn't permanent. He'll be back in a couple of days, immunized up to the hilt and wearing a plague-proof suit. You'd better fill your bags while you have the chance."

I obeyed. When I came back from the shelves, my bags bulging with their insipid contents, he was still there. "Thanks a lot," I said. "How did you happen to show up just then?"

"Oh . . . Don't you know me?"

I looked at him carefully. I didn't think I had ever seen him before. "No," I said at last.

"Ah," he answered. He turned and walked toward the open door. "Don't be too long about it," he said over his shoulder. "There's not much more time."

"Too long about what?" I asked. But he was already outside, and didn't turn back.

Well, I had plenty of food. When I got back to my pad I opened a can of the stuff. There were still a few cans with tastier contents, but I thought I had better get used to this. After I had finished eating, I read for a while and then went to bed.

I passed a restless night. I kept dreaming of Kyra, confused and disturbed dreams that were not quite nightmares. Somebody else was in the dreams, but I did not know who it was.

On the job next morning, I kept wondering about the grease-painted man. Perhaps he was right, and I did know him. Where had I seen him before?

Abruptly, about ten-thirty, when the blade of the bulldozer was pushing up a great wave of dirt, I realized what he had been talking about. I *had* seen him before, but he had been masked then. No wonder I hadn't recognized him.

He was the man with the horns who had scourged me on level H.

I jumped down from the bulldozer seat. With this bit of knowledge, another, even more valuable, had come: I knew who she was and where she had been waiting for me so long. And I was impatient now.

It didn't take me long to get to the warehouse where I had worked for so many months, moving stacks of boxes around. The middle-aged woman in the office looked up as I came in.

Our eyes met. There was no possible doubt.

I walked toward her. Her lips had begun to curve in a smile. "Why did you make me go so deep to look for you, Despoina?" I said.

16

SHE PUSHED the desk chair aside and came toward me. She was smiling, the faint, mysterious smile of archaic art. She put her right hand on my shoulder. "Blessed be," she said, and kissed me on the lips. "You had to find me as you did to be of use to me. Even the black-hilted sword must be forged."

I looked at her. Now that the confusion was gone from my eyes, I wondered that I could, even for a moment, have thought her middle-aged. It was partly a matter of make-up and partly a matter of acting. Despoina was an excellent actress, but there must have been a liberal dash of fith-fath for the illusion to be so complete. In actual fact she was, as I found out later, just two months younger than I myself.

"Kyra said you had been captured by the FBY," I said at last.

"Kyra said that at our direction," she answered. "We wanted you to stay quietly on F while she undertook your training. But you have been slow about remembering. We must hurry. *They* are enlarging and consolidating their power. There is not much time."

"What must we do?"

"Don't you know?"

I considered, half closing my eyes. Her perfume, delicate yet strong, came to me like the breath of an ethereal forest of cedar and sandalwood. "I think—" (It was like trying to read almost illegible writing) "I think we must go down to level H again.

"Before the FBY shut that level off," I went on, "they made a cursory examination of what they found there, and brought up all they considered valuable. But the heart of your work—your lab notes and extracts—they left behind, either because they did not find it at all, or because they did not realize its value. We must go after it. I don't know how I know this, though."

"Wicca are people who know things without being told," she said.

"How can we get down?" I asked. "Kyra said the level had been closed off, and I think it has. Is there another way down?"

"You must help with the answer to that."

Once more I considered. "We will have to scry to try to find it. That would be easy, if we could call our people together. But for so many people to be able to meet would certainly arouse suspicion. A man and woman could get away with it, I think."

"Yes, if a man and a woman are together an onlooker will think their purpose is sexual, provided they are not with each other too long. But we must have Ross to help us. It takes three."

"Ross?" I asked.

"The man who gave you the scourging. He has been taking your place."

"Taking my place? I don't understand."

She sighed. "Even now you don't know who you are. Well, that will come later. Now we must decide where to meet."

"On the edge, the east edge, of the old burial ground," I answered promptly. "Nobody goes there at night It ought to be safe."

Did a shadow pass over her face? But she answered that it was a good idea; she and Ross would meet me about eight, before the moon came up.

I looked into her greenish eyes, only a little below the level of mine. At this distance the make-up she used to age herself was obvious, and it was odd to see her radiant youth shining through it, like the moon breaking through clouds.

I touched her hair lightly with the tips of my fingers. "I wish I could see your real hair," I said. "Not this gray stuff."

"Later," she said, laughing. "You must go now, Sam. Somebody in the warehouse might get suspicious."

"All right." I turned to go.

At the door of the little office I looked back. She had drawn the illusion of age around her again, as a woman may put a scarf about her shoulders; in any case I wasn't in love with her. I was still half in love with my half-sister. But as I looked at her bending over some sort of form with a pencil in one hand, I realized that the sense of the future—troubling, ambiguous, dangerous, but *mine*—the sense of the future had come back to me.

I wasn't much use the rest of the day with the bulldozer. Once Jim yelled at me to get the lead out of my tail for Crissake, did I want Halley's comet to be back before I got that body buried? I kept thinking about Despoina—not as a lover thinks about a woman, but as an explorer speculates about the unknown heart of a continent. One thing I was perfectly sure of: she and I would be able to work together. This, if I had known it, is a matter taken very seriously in witchcraft circles.

I quit work at the usual time. Back at my pad, I had a shower with lots of soap, and put on all fresh clothes. I thought of eating, but I wasn't very hungry, and it struck me that if we were going to scry it might be better for me to have a relatively empty stomach.

I felt that some further preparations might be in order. I hunted through drawers and cupboards until I found, in the kitchen, a ball of white twine. It was so old that its strength was almost gone, but I braided it in three double strands, tying a knot at intervals, and slipped it into my pocket, satisfied. I would have liked to dye it red, but I couldn't find anything to dye it with.

I got to the rendezvous early. A row of some sort of monstrous misshapen vegetation—beets, I thought—shut out the sky on two sides of the field, but it lay open to the west, where something of the great light of evening yet lingered. I looked without hindrance into the abyss of air.

The skies were clearer now than they had been when I was a boy. Then, a pall of smoke from the busy works of men, forges and furnaces, would have lain along the horizon and reached halfway to the zenith. Was it a good thing, after all, that the plagues had come? The world had been veering helplessly toward disaster when the deaths of many had saved us from the death of all.

Suddenly I was overcome by a passion of homesickness, of longing for the world, not as it had been but as it could be. "I have such a longing for the republic!" the woman named Pilar had cried. And Cromwell, that godly politician, had had engraved on his sword, "For the commonwealth of England."

Fine talk, fine words. But the world never had been like that.

There was a noise behind me, and Despoina and Ross emerged from the shade of the monstrous leaves. Despoina carried a parcel in one hand. She was wearing a voluminous wrap of some thin stuff, with a fold pulled over her head, and if I had not been expecting her I would never have recognized her, for her hair seemed to be dark brown, and she looked to be about thirty. Ross had on mechanics' coveralls, and there was a smear of grease across his face.

They kissed me in greeting, he on the cheek, she on the lips. Despoina undid her parcel and showed us what it contained. Now that they were here, I realized how I had missed them, and how lonely for some of my own sort I had been. It was the same sense of identity and inner peace I had experienced with Kyra. We Wicca know how to be happy even in a bad world. But we are not content with a bad world.

The pale moon had begun to climb the sky. Despoina laid her wrap aside. She cast the circle and told us what to do. The rite began.

I cannot, of course, describe it. It must be remembered also that I was still not fully an initiate. Let it suffice to say that I could see nothing at all. The surface of the stone remained obdurately blank.

At least I had to confess defeat, I handed it to Ross, and he passed it on to Despoina, saying, "The moon looks down on everything."

She took the flat stone rather reluctantly, I thought, and stood for a moment holding it, as if wondering what to do. Then she laid it on the ground and began to undress, still rather hesitantly. It was not modesty, I knew, that made her hesitate, but a fear of attracting the attention of a possible passer-by. She had decided to risk it.

She tossed her clothing out of the circle, so she could move freely, and then held out her hand to me. I gave her the knotted cord in my pocket. She ran her hands along it, flicking her fingers at each knot. Ross was singing tonelessly, in a thin, quavering voice. She tied the cord around her head and picked up the stone.

For a while there was silence, except for Ross's quavered song. She kept breathing on the stone and wiping it off with her hand. The moon was higher now, and the pearly light glimmered along her shoulders and breasts and thighs.

At last she said, "There's a mist. I can't get rid of the mist. I wonder if they . . . Ross, you must try."

"All right." He stripped off his clothing and motioned to me to do likewise. After all, the risk of attracting undesired attention would not be significantly increased if we all three were naked, and it would make the scrying easier. I felt the cool night air along my skin.

She advanced toward Ross with a dancing step, moved around him twice "planetarily," and then gave him the stone. How different this was from how it would have been if all of us could have been together, and how much more difficult! All the same, the force was building up. I could feel it tingle along my forehead and run with a shiver into the spot in the pit of my stomach Kyra had called "the knot of power."

Ross began to stammer and jerk. "The—the—Oh, the—the—"

We seemed upon the edge of revelation. Ross gritted his teeth with a loud noise. Once more he stammered, "The—the—" Then he drew a deep sigh and began to sob as if his heart would break.

It was painful to hear him. Despoina's hands were clasped together rigidly under her breasts. There was nothing more to be hoped for. Our power had reached its highest point, and from now would only recede. I stooped for the black-hilted sword, which was lying on the ground in front of my feet, turned it toward me as best I could, and made three deep gashes with the unwieldly thing in the flesh of my chest.

Power flashed forth from freshly shed blood; the black stream ran down my belly and trickled along my thighs. And in that moment

Ross said quite loudly and clearly, "The pool. The pool with the glittering man."

He dropped the scrying stone and looked around him blankly. Then his knees buckled and he fell forward on his face.

Despoina clutched at me. "Get down," she whispered urgently. "Someone is coming." She threw herself down full length beside Ross.

I followed her. We lay tensely quiet. I could feel grains of earth sticking to the blood on my body, and had time to wonder whether anybody who invaded our crude circle would experience any of the odd psychic phenomena that sometimes occur. Then voices were heard along the road.

"You think that's the way, then?" somebody said.

"Absolutely, sir. You see, the first thing to do is to get some means of coercing them. But after that, sir, it will take something more."

"What?" said the first speaker keenly.

"Ah, that's the difficulty. But I think, sir, I'm on the right track. You see, sir, if they can be turned . . ."

The voices died away. We lay in the dirt for a considerable time longer. I was speculating on the fragmentary conversation we had overheard. From the tone of it, and the fact that the speakers had been so easy with each other, I thought they must have been FBY men. The general subject was plain enough. But what had the younger man meant by "if they can be turned"?

At last Despoina touched my arm. "We can get up now," she said. "They won't be back."

We all three got to our feet. Ross was yawning and shivering. "Did I say anything?" he asked. "I don't remember what happened between when you gave me the stone and when I heard voices along the road dying away."

"Yes, you said something," she told him. "You said, 'The pool. The pool with the glittering man.'"

"Is that all?" He sounded disappointed.

We had pulled on our clothes. The rite must have taken longer than I had thought, or we had lain a longer time on the ground, for the moon was now in the western sky. The east was still impenetrably dark, but with the darkness that forebodes dawn.

"I don't know what I meant," Ross continued. "It doesn't make any sense to me. 'The pool with the glittering man.' No, I don't know what I meant."

"I think I do," I said suddenly. I had been tucking my shirttail into my trousers. The blood was sticky on my chest. "I've done a lot of wandering around in the levels, you know. There's a pool like that high up in the natural caves, on B."

Despoina nodded. "We must go there," she said.

"Yes." I looked toward the east. It was very slightly lighter than it had been. Once more I must exchange the sun for the depths where it is always light.

17

B IS far too close to the surface for the purple fungus to grow there. It was designed as a mass shelter against blast, for the thousands and thousands of city dwellers who weren't to be permanently domiciled in the deeper levels. It consists of an apparently interminable series of interlacing arched arcades, part natural and part artificial, with shop fronts. The shops have never been occupied. I suppose the idea was that people would while away the time they were in the mass shelter by buying souvenirs to take back to the radioactive surface with them. Perhaps I wrong the designers by imputing to them anything so egg-headed as an idea. They designed as they were told.

I got to the pool ahead of the others. When we had parted on the edge of the burial grounds, an hour or two before, I had given them careful directions how to find it. We had decided not to wait for evening to try to discover the way down to H. Time was getting short, and we thought we could all three be absent from our jobs without arousing immediate suspicion. Absenteeism was common enough.

The pool itself is in one of the peripheral arcades, beside a store window. The designer had taken advantage of the natural drip from the rock roof above to install an ornamental pool, blue-lined, complete with goldfish. The glittering man is inside the pool.

I stood looking over the edge at him. He lay face down in the water, a heavily built man in a gray business suit, with a briefcase in the water by his side. Goldfish swam over and around him, and brushed against the hard tendrils of his hair.

The water must have had an extraordinarily high mineral content, for the man in the pool looked as if he had been dipped in sugar candy, the kind with the big hard bright crystals all over it. He was as brilliant as a dime-store diamond. He glittered like an old-fashioned Christmas card.

I was struck by a haunting familiarity in the outlines of his head and neck. Surely, despite the way the coat of crystals blurred his shape, it seemed that I had seen him somewhere before.

Overcoming a considerable distaste, I plunged my hands into the cold water and turned him face up. He moved easily, with only a little ripple and splash. His dead, bright face looked into mine.

I stepped back, wiping my wet hands on my trousers. Know him? Of course I did. He had been televised and photographed a lot when I was a boy. It was Hellman, one of the top weapons experts of pre-plague days. He had come to an unlikely place to die.

How had he died? I didn't think it was from plague; he didn't look like a plague victim, but he might have taken refuge on B from the plague. Probably he had had a heart attack and collapsed into the pool. I remembered having heard somewhere, ten years or so ago, that Hellman had a weak heart.

At any rate, he had avoided the terrible loneliness of the dead, for the little goldfish swam all about him and kept him company.

I heard a footfall. Despoina was walking toward me, once more in the guise of a middle-aged woman. She looked more tired than her make-up would warrant, and I realized, not only from my own fatigue, what an exhausting business "magic" is.

"Here comes Ross," she said when she had greeted me. "I think he may be going to treat us to a quotation. He has a Shakespearean look on his face."

Ross was, indeed, coming toward us from the other direction. "Hail to thee. Thane of Cawdor," he said as he came up to me. "The earth hath bubbles, as the water has, and these are of them." He looked down at the pool. "My word, he does glitter," he observed. "Why, it's Hellman! I'd know that jutting jaw and heavy jowls any-where. How did he happen to come here to die?"

"He must have been trying to get down to H," Despoina answered. "Perhaps he was trying to get away from the plague, or wanted to set up some sort of government down there. The president died early in the plague. And Hellman was an arrogant man."

"Whatever his motive was, here he is," Ross said. "I don't see how he expected to get down, though. This seems to be a perfectly ordinary pool."

I had been absently watching the movements of the goldfish. There was something oddly regular in the paths their swimming took. One group seemed, as far as I could judge, to mark out a series of figure eights, and another moved around the pool in a large ellipse.

I bent over and put one hand out directly in the path of an oncoming fish. It did not move aside or try to avoid my fingers. I closed my hand over it, brought my hand up through the water, and held out my catch on my palm for the other two to look at. All this time there was not a wriggle or a twitch from the fish.

We exchanged glances. "It's not alive," Despoina said. She poked it with one finger. "Metal, or plastic with a metallic coat. What makes it move, then, Sam?"

I said slowly, "if something is tracing out lines of force on the underside of the pool. . ."

Ross's eyes lit up. "I've seen something like that. . . . Wait—yes, I know now. There's a matter transmitter under the bottom of the pool."

"There must be some way of draining out the water," Despoina said practically. "But before you look for it, Sam, get his briefcase out and put it somewhere safe."

"Briefcase? Why?"

"Don't you remember his saying, just before the plagues broke out, that he and his staff had developed a portmanteau bomb?"

"You think he's got one of them in the briefcase?"

"Of course. Hellman wouldn't go anywhere without a sample of the most advanced weaponry. He was like a man in love who always carries something to remind him of his girl."

Ross reached down into the water, picked up the briefcase carefully by its handle, and pulled it out. It was coated with the same coruscating crystals that covered Hellman.

"Come along, fatal instrument," Ross said to the briefcase. He carried it across to the store front, opened the door, and laid the case down respectfully inside. "I hope nobody bothers it," he said. "After ten years in the water, it still might be able to sting."

Despoina had knelt down beside the pool, her hands over her eyes in the way that was familiar to me from Kyra. "I see something," she said. "Knobs and gauges. Help me, Sam."

I did as she was doing. Immediately the side of the pool, under its skin of plastic, leaped into sight. There were the gauges of which she had spoken, pipes of two sizes, and a tiny pump, nestled into a niche in the rough rock.

I turned my eyeless vision toward the bottom of the pool. Here, underneath the plastic lining, was a broad flat surface, patterned in small black and white squares, like a mosaic. It was difficult to be sure of the color of any individual square; black was white and then white again. But the outlines of the pattern were plain enough—two overlapping figure eights, set inside a large ellipse.

It didn't look much like my idea of a matter transmitter; but the craft, while it gives its lovers much, does not make them electronics experts or give them an intuitive grasp of neo-nuclear physics. But something, at any rate, could be done with the side of the pool.

"Have you a screwdriver?" I asked Ross.

"Sure. Never go anywhere without one." He pulled the tool out of a loop on his coveralls and handed it to me.

I pried with it in three places along the line where the blue plastic met the raised rock edge. There was no visible crack in the plastic itself, but on the third pry a large section of the plastic came out, leaving the gauges and pump easily accessible.

"Hmm," said Ross. He leaned over the side, twiddled with the pump for a moment, and then touched a lever. The level of the water in the pool began to recede.

"What's it like under the plastic floor?" he asked me.

"Can't you see it?" I replied, surprised.

"No. I haven't got that kind of sight."

I described it for him. He listened, nodding occasionally, while the water ebbed and the metallic goldfish sank lower and lower in it.

"It's a matter transmitter, for sure," he said when I had finished. "Mono-terminal type. We might try it on Hellman, to be sure it's still okay. That stuff gets out of fix easy, and it's been ten years anyhow since it was used."

He jumped down into the pool, now completely empty, beside the body of the glittering man. Here, at his ease, he adjusted controls, turned dials, and did some intense, frowning work with a pair of jeweler's pliers.

"Doesn't the plastic lining of the pool have to come out?" Despoina asked, from above him.

"No. It won't get transmitted. It's not really here, you see. That's why the water could be pumped out through it."

He hauled himself back up over the side of the pool. The goldfish had settled down on the plastic along the lines of force from below, where they twitched uneasily.

"No, it's not quite right," Ross said, sighting down at Hellman's body. He jumped down into the pool again, moved Hellman a couple of inches, and then came back to where Despoina and I were standing. "The attempt and not the deed Confounds us," he said. He reached over the edge of the pool and pressed a switch.

For an instant nothing at all happened. Then Hellman's body began to rotate.

He turned slowly at first, and then faster and faster. He shot off sparks of light, he turned like a Catharine wheel, he sent up gushes of splendor like a skyrocket. It was incredible, it dazzled our eyes painfully. Then, with one last great coruscation of fire, he blazed up and was gone. There was a smell like burning resin in the air.

"Whew!" said Ross. He pulled out a bandana and wiped his face. He reached down and shut off the switch. "Good job we tried it on him first. There's something wrong with the adjustment. It oughtn't to do that."

I am, as I said, no expert on neo-nuclear physics, but it struck me that the voltage was too great, and I told Ross so. Despoina listened to our technicalities, a faint smile on her lips.

"The voltage may have something to do with it," she said after I had talked Ross around to agreeing that the voltage should be reduced. "But bring the goldfish up and put them on the floor beside the pool. They were not in the water merely for ornament."

Ross and I obeyed her. There were eighteen of the light, hard objects, and they seemed to be of two sorts—larger ones, with the body bronzy and the gills white; and smaller ones, all of bright metallic gold. Even seen up close, they were convincing imitations of fish.

Despoina bent over the artificial fish absorbedly. She picked them up one at a time and put them down in a pattern, stopping often to consider. It reminded me of things I had seen Kyra do. At last she sat back on her heels and looked up at us. "That's about it, I think."

I looked at what she had made. It was a pattern almost identical with a certain witches' mark. "Despoina, were the men who built the transmitter members of the craft?"

"No, almost certainly not. I didn't arrange the fish in that pattern because I thought they were. But the pattern is a means of manipulating physical reality, and it's valid with no relation to who uses it. Try transmitting something, Ross, and see if it works."

"What?" Ross asked. "It ought to be something about the size and mass of a human body, to be significant. And we've already used Hellman up."

"Aren't there any planks inside the store?" Despoina asked. "Some sort of shelving? That might do."

Ross and I brought out three six-foot planks and laid them along the bottom of the pool. They did not look at all like a human body, but they might have about the same mass. "But in them nature's copy's not eterne," said Ross, whose mind seemed to be running on *Macbeth*. "I'll step down the voltage." He applied the screwdriver.

"That's the best I can do," he said finally. "All set? Let's try it. Now."
Once more he pressed down the switch.

The planks disappeared. I was looking toward the far end of the
pool, and I saw a faint sparking of light at the moment the switch was
depressed. But that was all. Except for that, there was no display. The
planks had simply disappeared.

"Seems to be okay," said Ross. He shut the machinery off. "Well,
who's going first?"

"I am," I said. I wasn't frightened, but my breath was coming a
little fast.

Despoina frowned. "There's nothing more to be done with the
machinery, I suppose," she said, "but I think there might be something more to be done for Sam and me before Ross tries to transmit
us. I mean some sort of pre-processing. The planks seemed to go
all right. But a plank's not a human being. If we could—What's that
noise?"

Footsteps—hurried, almost running—were coming toward us
along the arcade. I whirled toward the sound, my heart in my mouth.
That the three of us were together would be immediately suspicious,
and on top of that we were patently engaged in some unusual activity. If the approaching person was somebody with FBY connections,
we'd be taken off for questioning at once; if it was merely some private person, he was likely enough to report us, if only for the purpose of currying favor with the "new government."

The runner came into view. I saw with astonishment that it was
Kyra. She was making good speed, for all her high-heeled slippers,
and she had a small satchel, like a doctor's bag, in one hand.

"Blessed be," she said breathlessly when she got up to us. Her
words were almost tumbling over each other. "I came to help you.
You must hurry, Despoina and Sam. The FBY is hunting you."

18

I HAD a sudden fancy to ask Despoina to let down her hair. I had never seen it in a good light, burning and beautiful, let alone being able to touch and handle it; and if the FBY was going to capture us in the next few minutes, I probably never would have an opportunity to see it. It seemed a pity. But before I could make my request, the two women began to talk hurriedly.

"How do you know they are hunting us?" Despoina asked. "Are you sure?"

"Yes, I'm sure," Kyra answered. "I was on my way from F to help you—I knew you needed me—when I heard voices. This was on the edge of level D. I couldn't get sight of the speakers, and this in itself made me suspicious, for you know *they* have some of our techniques, and understand how to foil the seeing.

"I hid in the lower gallery. I was a long way from them, but the gallery has odd acoustical properties, and I could hear them talking as plainly as if I'd been standing at their sides.

"They said 'the man Sewell and his woman' must have been warned, but that they—the FBY—were going to look for them from the other end. They used your name, Despoina. But they pronounced it wrong."

While she was talking, Kyra had been opening her little black satchel, getting out two clinical thermometers, and shaking them down. Now she popped a thermometer into my mouth and into Despoina's.

"Where had they been looking for us?" Despoina asked in a muffled voice.

"On F, I think. They seemed to have me and Despoina mixed up, and to think Sam had been staying down there with her. I must just have missed them on my way up from F. From what they said, they didn't know anything at all about that raid the disposal people made."

Kyra took my wrist and began to count my pulse. I said, around the thermometer, "Where are they looking for us now?"

"I think they're going to try to pick up your trail from the bulldozer crew, Sam. They said something about a 'trace receptor.' Then they got too far away for me to hear any more. But there's no doubt they're after you with all they've got."

She plucked the thermometers out of our mouths, read them, and nodded. Then she took Despoina's pulse. Here, too, the result must have been satisfactory, for she nodded again.

"Now, listen," Kyra told us swiftly. "In transmitting anything as complex as a human being, the mental attitude is of the highest importance. A person isn't like a block of wood that can get scrambled around a bit in transmission and still get there as itself. For a person to get through to the other end satisfactorily, he must keep his mind *inside* himself, inside his body. Despoina knows what I mean. Sam, do you remember that lesson I gave you with the box?"

I nodded. "Yes. I wasn't very good at it."

"You've got to be better this time," Kyra said grimly. "Concentrate! Don't let anything distract you. Pull your mind *inside.*"

She got a bottle from her medicine bag, opened it, and handed us each a capsule. "These will help. They're a drug psychiatrists used to use to combat depersonalization. Swallow them."

Despoina and I obeyed. Kyra looked at me for a moment, frowning. "Sam had better have something else," she said. "Here."

She gave me a tiny blue tablet. It left a haunting bitterness in my gullet. "Now, lie down in the pool on your backs, side by side," she said. "Ross will want to adjust you. I don't understand the mechanics of transmission, only the medical conditioning."

Despoina and I lay down side by side. I could smell her delicate perfume intermittently. Ross was squinting down at us and telling us to move an inch one way or another. It was a little like being in bed with her, and a little like getting ready to have our picture taken.

At last Ross had us adjusted to his satisfaction. "May I hold her hand?" I called up to him.

"Sure. Good idea." He made a final inspection of the gauges.

"Remember what I told you!" Kyra called. "It's im—"

"Come out with your hands high or we'll shoot!" a hard authoritative voice shouted. It seemed to be still some distance off.

The FBY, obviously. Before I could move or try to get up from my place beside Despoina, Ross yelled down at me, "Stay there, Sam! Don't move! Kyra and I'll be all right! Don't move!"

I saw him press the switch.

There was a terrible jar, as if the world had ended under me, and then blackness, blackness, nothing at all. Nothing at all.

In that last moment I had recalled Kyra's lesson and pulled my mind into myself. It was almost too late. When the blackness began to abate, for a long time "I" wandered.

I felt no pain, partly because I had no sense of personal identity, and partly because of the very nature of the experience. But there was an aching tedium, like the weary dreams of sickness and fever, a repellent and meaningless monotony of perception, even though it was not an "I" who perceived.

It was a space, a time of gray flitting shapes, as colorless as granite. They were not shadows, for they were all of one uniform gray, and they were oddly flat, like silhouettes made of paper. I never saw them edge-on, but I was always aware of their flatness. They moved through me, or I through them, restlessly and tediously.

I was always alone. I had been holding Despoina's hand when Ross pressed the switch, but she was not there—nobody was there—in the gray. I had no feeling of having lost her; I was too depersonalized to suffer a sense of loss. There was nothing where I was but the flat implausible shapes and their interminable movement and appearing.

Despoina, she told me later, had experienced almost exactly the same weary confusion and movement of gray silhouettes as I had. What had happened, I think, was that Krya had failed to appreciate the extent to which the operation of the transmitter would be affected, with reference to both Despoina and me, by my mental attitude. Kyra had thought I would be the only one affected. Actually, Despoina was as unable as I to help me or herself.

We might have wandered forever through our separate limbos, through the dreary shapes that interpenetrated us, if it had not been for a lucky accident. (In the craft, we say that luck tends to be deserved.) Or rather, a pair of lucky accidents, since the activities of the man we were later to know as "the fat rat" certainly had something to do with it. But in the main, Despoina and I owed our preservation to the fact that, up on level B where gunfire was going on, a bullet went wild.

One of the attackers was firing at Kyra, who had taken cover inside the vacant store. He missed, and his bullet went pinging into the plastic side of the pool, a few inches above the tesselations of the scanner. The bullet jarred the whole transmitter, with the result that, for a micro-second or two, it functioned at peak efficiency.

We, of course, were not aware of this. Ross made this explanation to me much later. What I felt was, through my endless tedium, a sudden, most welcome, accession of identity.

It was like the full moon breaking through broken clouds. I knew who I was, I knew I had a body, I clutched after it. From being a nothing who perceived without any sense of identity, I became a man who was anxiously, almost feverishly, pulling his mind inside his body so he might have something to perceive with. I drank up the sense of my own identity as a thirsty man drinks water.

I could feel my body now, and it was wonderful, it was glorious. I seemed to be holding onto something. I fought desperately for awareness of it. And then I realized, in a flood of joy, what it was: I was holding Despoina's hand.

That did it. With an almost palpable bump, I was out of the limbo of stone-colored shapes and back in the world of reality.

I sat up and looked around. Despoina, her knees a little flexed, was lying beside me. I caught a glimpse of tesselations under her that faded as I looked. She sat up too, squeezed my hand, and smiled.

We were in a tiny, stone-walled room, with an opening in one side. One wall was covered by an enormous photo montage of the moon. The light that came through the window opening looked like daylight. Close beside us on the floor were the three big planks Ross had sent through the transmitter ahead of us.

"Well, here we are," I said. My voice sounded remote and weak.

Despoina nodded. She got to her feet, went over to the opening, and looked through it. Then she came back and sat down beside me on the floor.

She had said nothing at all; her expression had not changed, and yet I felt a premonition of disaster. Slowly her hand went to her head, and she took off the covering—part turban, part wig—she had used to conceal her hair. It streamed down over her shoulders like molten copper, beautiful and alive. It seemed to fill the small stone room with its light.

Still she was silent. I had time to notice how the color of her hair made her skin look dazzlingly white. At last she raised her head and looked directly into my eyes.

I waited for her to speak. "This isn't level H," she said at last.

19

I HAD known she was going to say that. I shook my head to clear it. I still had the sense of sliding, interpenetrating planes of gray just outside my field of sight. I said, "Where are we, then? On the moon?"

She laughed. "No, not the moon," she answered. "It looks like the surface, but—go see for yourself, Sam."

I went over to the window. It was a small unglazed opening, like a window in a castle, with a broad stone sill. Through it I saw a landscape on a day of high haze. There was a gently curving road of white gravel in the foreground, with small private houses on either side. Off to the left and further away there was a supermarket with a big parking lot, and what seemed to be a school. In the far distance a line of rolling tree-grown hills shut off the view.

Something in the scene struck me as unnatural, and after a moment I realized what it was: the trees. We couldn't be on the surface, then. Was this another vast underground cavern, like level G, so big that it could contain trees and a range of hills?

This seemed wildly improbable. I looked more closely, squinting out at the view, and suddenly something clicked in my mind. What I was looking at was a miniature landscape, an illusory panorama, most cunningly arranged and contrived.

There were plenty of clues, once I got onto it. For instance, the supermarket was just a little too big to be at the distance it apparently was, and the grass in front of the houses was too coarse. The absence of any movement in the landscape was another giveaway. But it was an excellent illusion. Much care and attention had been spent on it.

I told Despoina my discovery, finishing, "I think we're still underground."

She nodded. "I think so too. It *feels* underground.... Are you worried about Kyra and Ross?"

"Why—yes, I guess I am."

"So am I. I can't pick up their minds. See if you can help."

I joined my mind to hers, but without success. Telepathy is always a chancy method of communication, and now there was something blocking it.

Despoina sighed. "We must hope they're all right. Let's try to find out where we are."

We opened the rough wooden door and walked into a short corridor. Here three or four other doors confronted us. A deep humming seemed to come from behind the nearest one.

Despoina threw it open. We saw a large, a very large room—it seemed half the size of a skating rink—that was as full of electrical equipment as a power company sub-station. The air was loud with its noise.

I was about to close the door again, when I saw, at the far end of the big room, a flicker of moving cloth. Somebody was tending the machinery.

"Hi, there!" I yelled. "You down there! Hello!"

There was no answer, but I heard, a second later, the noise of hurrying feet and the slamming of a door.

With Despoina at my heels, I ran toward the sound. There was nobody there, and when we opened the door that had just been slammed, we found we were in another corridor, a longer one, with six doors opening out of it. No one was in the corridor.

Despoina and I looked at each other. I selected one of the doors at random and found we were in a perfect maze of partitioned rooms and cubbyholes. There were shelves and storage space everywhere. None of it was occupied.

We made our way back to the corridor. I opened the other doors and found, in turn, that one of them hid a shallow supply closet; one gave on another very long corridor with more doors; one on an elaborate cache of tinned and canned desserts; one opened on a bunk room for four, apparently never occupied; and the last on a tiled shower and lavatory. It seemed hopeless.

"Let's try to pick him up with the seeing," Despoina suggested.

We tried, but the attempt was as fruitless as our attempt to contact Ross and Kyra telepathically had been. For some reason which I do not understand even now—I recommend it to the curiosity of future investigators—our distance senses were useless here. (We Wicca do not consider "the seeing" extra-sensory.) All we got was blackness and a touch of vertigo.

We were getting worried. We didn't know where we were or how to get away from there, and the urgency of our need to get to H was more acute than ever. At last Despoina said, "We ought to set a trap."

"What could we bait it with?" I asked.

"Well, the person we saw in the room with the machinery obviously isn't curious. There's no point to doing something to appeal to his curiosity. But he was working on the machinery. Suppose we disabled one of the generators? Wouldn't that bring him running to see what was wrong?"

It was a good idea. Inside the generator room, I fixed a length of wire across the opening of the door through which the unknown might be expected to enter. It was meant as a trip-up. Then I took a screwdriver and scraped a handful of good-sized grit from one of the rock walls. I tossed the grit into the armature of the biggest of the generators.

There was a shower of bright sparks. The happy hum of machinery changed to a harsh note of protest. The grinding lasted for only an instant. Then there was a big puff of black smoke. I smelled ozone in the air.

The fluorescent panels in the ceiling had dimmed perceptibly. "That ought to bring him," I said. "I hope he's got an auxiliary generator stashed away somewhere."

We settled ourselves on either side of the door to wait. The cuts on my chest were bleeding a little; I could feel the blood trickling down through the hair.

The semi-twilight was soothing, and I had had a sleepless night. I tried to keep awake, but I think I dozed. I was roused by Despoina taking my hand.

"Listen," she breathed. "Somebody's coming."

There was a noise of flapping footsteps, and an indistinct muttering. The unknown seemed to be talking to himself.

The sounds drew nearer. I waited tensely, my muscles taut. The door opened. There was a heavy thud. The unknown had fallen to the floor.

I pounced on him before he could move. He did not resist me at all. He had fallen on his face, and he lay so quietly that I thought he might be badly hurt. But he was still talking, I didn't know whether to me or to himself.

"Get up," I said finally. I helped him to his feet.

My eyes had grown accustomed to the dim light, and I could see him pretty well. He was wearing a purplish dressing gown, with a scarf tucked in at the neck, and he looked like my idea of Ratty in *The Wind in the Willows*. Both his forehead and his chin receeded. He was definitely fat. Dark glasses covered his eyes.

"Why didn't you stay in the moon room?" he asked petulantly. His voice was faded and high. "You were supposed to stay there. You're to be transshipped."

20

DURING THE time we were in contact, he never looked directly at either of us, but always at a point an inch or two above our heads. It made him disconcerting to deal with.

"Transshipped? Where to?" I asked. "To the moon?"

He was silent. Only, seemingly without thinking, he put out a long pale tongue and licked his lower lip and chin.

"We want to get to level H," I said. I was holding him by the collar of his dressing gown. Without precisely meaning to do it, I gave him a vigorous shake.

He ignored the shake. "To level H!" He laughed. "I can make a better level H than any *you're* likely to find."

"What do you mean by that?"

"Didn't you see my pictures?" He sounded surprised. (It was the only thing he ever did seem surprised at; he took our presence in his territory, and my ruin of the generator, with perfect calm.) "There's one of them outside the window of the moon room. You must have noticed it. I've made dozens of them."

He fumbled in the pocket of his dressing gown and brought out a tiny model of a service-station gas pump. "This is one I'm working on," he said, holding it for us to see. "I don't know yet what to use for the hose, though."

He put the model back carefully in his pocket. From the other pocket he extracted a flat cooky and began munching on it.

"After I get the service station done, I'll make another supermarket," he said around the crumbs.

"Do you like desserts?" Despoina asked him. She had put a cajoling note in her voice.

"Yes. Don't you?" He finished the cooky and began on another one.

"You've got to help us get down to level H," I told him as sternly as I could. Actually, I felt foolish saying anything at all to him; it was like talking to a cream puff.

He shook his head. "Impossible," he said, addressing the air above me. "That's not what my instructions say."

"Where are you supposed to send us?" I asked.

"Harris wanted to go to the moon. That's why he put up that montage. But he wound up as a technician on level F."

"How long ago was this?" I asked, still trying to get at something definite.

"I don't know. A week or two. No, it might be years. I've made a lot of models since then."

Despoina said, "Wouldn't it be easier to help us to level H than to transship us?"

"I guess so. But my instructions don't say that."

"*We* like desserts too," I said, trying to be severe. "We love them. If you don't help us down to H, we'll eat them all up."

"*All* up?" He sounded doubtful.

"All of them. You know there aren't any too many left."

"Oh!" He got another cooky from his pocket and popped it, whole, into his mouth. "All right. If there's trouble, I'll say it was your fault. But that man"—he meant me—"will have to install the auxiliary generator." His words were muffled, but audible enough.

This seemed reasonable. Under his direction, I lugged over a smallish generator from a closet in the next corridor and installed it. He kept a jealous eye on my movements and on Despoina. I could see he feared for the safety of his cache of desserts.

When the generator was installed, he said, "I haven't done this for a long time. I'd better try sending something to H before I send you."

The light had got back to normal since the power output was restored. I tried to catch his eye, but he wouldn't look at me. Still, there didn't seem any especial reason why he should be lying. I said, "What are you going to send?"

"Those planks that came before you did," His head was tilted far back, and his eyes were fixed on the ceiling. Following his gaze, I saw that a viewing plate was set overhead, where the floor and sides of the moon room were visible.

Ratty opened the front of a console and began twiddling with dials. "You two go move the planks so their long axis is parallel with the door, with a margin of about two feet around them," he told us. "Then come back here."

We obeyed. I think we were both nervous, for it was certainly possible that he would take advantage of our being in the moon room to send us anywhere at all to get rid of us. But nothing happened, and we got back to the generators all right.

Old Fat Rat had pulled a piece of peg board forward, and was laying out a design on its surface with metal clips. The design closely resembled the one Despoina had constructed with the fish at the poolside. Then he put wires in the clips and strung the wires back in the same design.

"What a lot of trouble this is," he said; "almost as much trouble as sending you to . . ." His high voice died away, and he got another cooky, a filled one this time, out of his pocket. He munched on it with his eyes half closed. Then, licking his lips, he pressed a switch.

Despoina and I were both looking at the viewing plate. A pattern of moving squares had become dimly visible on the floor where the planks did not cover it. The squares pursued each other monotonously for at least four or five minutes, without anything more happening. I yawned involuntarily as I watched them.

Suddenly the plate grew dark. Then it seemed to explode into a billow of light brown.

What had happened? The billow of light brown stayed on the viewing plate. It didn't resemble anything I was familiar with. "Let's go see what it is," I suggested at last.

The three of us, old Fat Rat flapping along in his bedroom slippers, went out into the corridor. I opened the door of the moon room, and what was inside came puffing out.

We had jumped back, but it was quite harmless. It was a mass of fluffy wood shavings, a little coarser than the stuff the British used to call woodwool, and the Americans, unaccountably, excelsior. I looked inside the moon room, and saw that it was filled, filled to the ceiling, with the shavings. This, then, was what had become of the planks Ratty had attempted to transmit.

"I must have done something wrong," he said unnecessarily, looking over our heads. He popped a candy—peppermint, from the smell of it—into his mouth. "If you'll clear that woody stuff out of the way, I'll transmit you to H."

There was no need for Despoina and me to exchange glances. Entrusting ourselves to Ratty's ministrations was obvious madness. He might have been a good mechanic once, but time and loneliness had long ago eroded his competence.

"Isn't there any other way to get to H besides the transmitter?" I demanded.

He closed his eyes and sucked voluptuously on his peppermint.

I was wondering whether I should hit him, threaten to destroy his cache of desserts, or try flattery, when Despoina said in my ear, "Grab him from behind, Sam, and hold his head so he has to look at me."

Fat Rat was standing with his back half turned to me. I threw one arm around his body, pinning his hands to his sides, and with my other hand pressed down on the top of his head. He was puffy to the touch, like a marshmallow, and he smelled stale.

Despoina stepped in front of him, fumbling at the neck of her dress. She brought out something dangling at the end of a fine gold chain. It was her ring, the ring I had gone into the depths once before to take to her.

She unfastened the chain and began to swing the ring back and forth in an arc before Ratty's eyes. I could feel his head moving a very little from side to side as he followed the motion of the ring.

"Now," she said after a while, "what do you see?"

"Nothing."

"What do you see?"

"A man," he answered reluctantly.

"What else?"

"Big animals with horns."

"And the man?"

"He's running away from them. They're getting nearer. Oh, the poor man!"

She swung the ring some more. "Who is the man?" she asked in a voice not much louder than a whisper.

"I don't know"—this with a sort of desperate firmness.

"You know. Who is the man?"

His whole body shuddered. "It's me! It's me! Help, help!"

She stopped the motion of the ring with one finger. "What is the other way to H?" she asked.

". . . I don't know."

Once more the ring began to swing. "What is happening to the man?" she asked in a slow voice.

"Stop the swinging! I'll tell you anything you want! Help, help!" His sides heaved.

She stopped the ring again. "What is the way to H?"

"Fifth door to your right in the long corridor," he said. His voice was weak.

I let him go, and he sagged back against the wall. He looked as if he were going to have some sort of fit.

Despoina and I watched him for a moment. After a while he drew a deep sigh and wiped his face with the sleeve of his dressing gown. "I want some dessert," he said in a feeble voice.

I put my hand under his arm and steered him through the generator room and out into the other corridor. Here he tottered over to the cupboard that held his dessert cache.

He got out a big round tin of English biscuits. His hands were trembling. "Are you all right?" I asked him but he didn't seem to hear.

Obviously nothing more was to be hoped or expected from him. There were a lot of questions left unanswered—for instance, why he'd preferred trying to send us to H by matter transmitter to telling us about the door—but I didn't think we'd ever find out the answers to them.

Despoina and I opened the door that led to the long corridor. I looked back toward Ratty. He was leaning up against the wall, his eyes mildly glazed, opening the tin of English biscuits. As I watched, his long tongue came out and licked at the crumbs on his chin.

21

"WHAT WAS that?" I asked as we walked down the corridor.

"The business with the ring? Dwym-dight—soul paining. Our law forbids it except in the gravest emergencies. Even then, the elders in council should meet and approve. *I'm* not above the law."

I thought she might have said more, but by then we had reached the fifth door. I opened it, and we both walked inside.

We were in a largish room, with a good dozen of Ratty's panoramas installed in niches around the walls. There was a view of a walled medieval city, probably Carcassonne, a splendid lunar landscape with the earth rising on the right, and a very sandy desert, harboring two camels and a palm tree. The other panoramas were more conventional. All were beautifully done, and I found time to wonder fleetingly what Ratty had been in surface life, before he took up tending matter transmitters.

The center of the room held something quite different—a square stone coping, about two feet high and level on top, enclosing a space some five feet on a side. It looked like the coping around an old-fashioned well. A slight wind seemed to be blowing from the sides of the room toward it.

I approached the coping and looked over. I have only a fair head for heights; I was queasy instantly. I was looking down into a bottomless pit.

"Bottomless," of course, is not strictly accurate. All I mean is that I could see no bottom. The sides drew together with distance and became indistinct. They were pale blue at the top; I could not see their color further down. It was like looking from the top of the Empire State Building down a narrow shaft.

I held out my arm over the opening. Instantly, my hand and forearm jerked up—not because anything had pulled on them, but for the same reason that someone, lifting an unexpectedly light object, jerks it up in the air. My muscles were braced to withstand the ordinary pull of gravity on my arm, and that pull had abruptly diminished to about a tenth of itself.

Despoina had been watching. Now she went to one of Ratty's panoramas and came back with her hands full of miniature buildings and pieces of scenery. She dropped them into the shaft.

They fell slowly. We followed them with our eyes as long as we could see them, and still they seemed to be only drifting down.

I swallowed. I didn't like this at all. But there seemed to be no help for it. "I think it's an anti-grav," I said to Despoina. "I'm going to let myself down."

I sat on the edge of the coping for a minute, getting up my nerve. Then I turned around slowly, letting my body down into the shaft, while I still held onto the coping with my hands.

I felt a fantastic lightness. The air seemed to buoy me up like water; it was no effort at all to sustain my body in the shaft. Indeed, I felt that I could float upward if I wanted to.

"I think it's all right," I told Despoina. "I weigh a tenth of what I usually do, but my body offers just as much resistance to the air as usual. It's like being a ball of crumpled-up newspaper."

She nodded and unhesitatingly let herself down over the curb beside me. We hung for a moment. "Now!" I said, and we both let go.

I felt an instant of acute fear. But we were drifting down in the gentlest of katabases, the pale blue light around us, in almost pneumatic bliss, and we didn't accelerate. It was a very superior anti-grav.

I caught her hand and held it. The pale light was steady, and I could see her clearly. Her white dress and her red hair floated around her lightly, buoyed up by the air. I didn't know what we were falling toward, but I felt remarkably close to her. I would have been willing to go on falling like this for a long time.

"Despoina," I said, "what did you mean when you said, 'I'm not above the law'?"

"That there have been . . . witches who thought they were."

"Who? You must have meant somebody."

I could feel her considering whether to speak. "Kyra," she said at last.

"Kyra? My half-sister? What did she do?"

"We didn't know whether to admire her or to punish her. Kyra . . . loosed the yeasts."

I didn't understand what she meant immediately. Then I thought what an odd revelation this was to be made under these particular circumstances—silence, pale light, and Despoina and I descending gently together toward the end of our quest. I said, "You mean that Kyra was responsible for the outbreak of the plagues? I don't believe it. It's impossible."

"No, it's true. Kyra was a medical student then, in her last year of school. She was working part time as a lab assistant, to help with her expenses.

"The laboratory she was working in was under contract with the government, investigating fungi for possible use in biological warfare. One day Kyra found a cage of guinea pigs dying with something they hadn't been infected with. It was the pulmonary form of the plague.

"Kyra should have destroyed them at once, or have called in her superior to decide what was to be done. She didn't. She made cultures of the spores and released them. People began to die. And then the pulmonary mutated into the neurolytic form of the plague."

My face must have shown my shock, for Despoina said hurriedly, "Consider the situation, Sam. Have you forgotten? Nuclear war seemed absolutely inevitable. Nobody knew from day to day—from hour to hour—when it would begin. We lived in terror, terror which was sure to accomplish itself. Nobody even dared to hope for a quick death.

"Kyra realized what had come into her hands. She acted. She took on her shoulders a terrible responsibility; she assumed a dreadful guilt. She knew that plagues are never *universally* fatal. She decided it was better that nine men out of ten should die, than that all men should."

Still I was silent. Despoina went on, still defensively, "Was she wrong, Sam? Can we really think so? Some people did survive. And Kyra had no reason to believe she was immune. She risked her own life just as much as anyone's else."

"She broke the law, though," I said finally.

"Yes, the witch law. Such a decision should never have been made without the concurrence of the elders. So there had to be a punishment."

"Was that why she was sent to level F?"

"Yes. She hasn't been there constantly, though—only for the last three years. She was resentful at first. Her time of exile is nearly done now. Soon she can come back to the surface again."

I nodded. What a person Kyra was! Unhesitatingly she had taken on her young shoulders—she couldn't have been over twenty at the time—the agony of a decision a god might have flinched from making. Mrs. Prometheus—I felt proud to be related to her.

The light had been dimming. Now it was almost dark. Our gentle descent continued, but from the feel of the air I thought we must be getting near the bottom of the shaft. I was quite unprepared, though, when Despoina called out loudly and suddenly, "Cover your eyes, Sam! The light!"

I obeyed, but I was a fraction of a second too late. A terrible light broke over my eyes.

It left me blinded. It was not only the intensity of the light—though that was bad enough—but an odd paralyzing quality it had. My optical apparatus was intact, but the nerves could transmit no messages.

My feet touched bottom. We had landed. I said to Despoina, "Can you see anything?"

"A little. I think I know where we are, though H is a big level. I'll try to lead you. I expect our sight will come back. They can't have meant to blind users of the anti-grav permanently, only long enough to let them disarm any hostile people coming in that way. Come on."

We began to stumble forward, Despoina holding my left hand and using her free arm to guide herself along the wall. The other time I had been on H, my eyes had been dazed with fever; now I was literally and actually blinded. To this day, I know little of what H was really like. The people I have asked about it, including Dess herself, are always cagey.

"Can you see any better?" I asked as we lurched along.

"A very little. But I think it's not much farther. We must be almost there."

We moved on for three hundred—five hundred feet more. Then Despoina opened a door and guided me inside. "My sight's coming back," I announced.

"Good. Mine is almost normal. Sit down on the bed, Sam. I know where our stuff is."

I felt behind me, located a padded surface, and let myself down on it. I heard the sound of drawers being opened. My vision was returning in patches—small bright areas separated by big stretches of dark. But I could see enough of the wall in front of me to realize that I was once more in the little room with the sagging American flag on the wall, and the desk with the battery of telephones. I had come back to the spot on H designed to safeguard the "one most precious Life." (He had probably not felt very precious toward the end; the military had done a lot of arm-twisting on him. Death must have come to him as rather a relief.)

The patches of perception in my field of vision grew larger, and suddenly the darkness was gone. I saw Despoina standing before me, her face radiant with triumph, holding something out to me in her hands.

"Is that what we've been hunting?" I asked. "Two bottles marked 'Anacin,' and a bottle of Tums?"

She laughed. I had never seen her look so glad. "The spores of the mutated fungus are in the Tums bottle," she said, "and the extracts we made from them are in the bottles marked 'Anacin.' I think we have enough just in the two bottles to allow everybody alive in the United States at present to have a substantial dose. The extracts are potent stuff.

"Put the bottles in your pockets, Sam. I haven't any way of carrying them."

"And the lab notes?" I asked. I was buttoning the Tums bottle in my right breast pocket.

"Here." She picked up a filing folder marked "Classified" and handed it to me.

I took the lab notes out—there were only four or five pages of them, on thin bond paper—and folded them up. I put them in my breast pocket with the Tums bottle. The two plastic bottles marked "Anacin" I bestowed separately, one in my left breast pocket, the other in my hip pocket, where I buttoned the flap.

Now that what we had come for was safely lodged on my person, I felt an intense relief. Not only had we attained our purpose, but also, if there should be more trouble with the FBY, we had something to bargain with.

And now one question was inescapably the next item on the agenda. Despoina and I had consciously shirked mentioning it to each other; now it had to be faced. How were we to get up to the surface again?

From the corridor I heard the tinkling of tiny bells.

22

THE SOUND of bells was coming from a man in the plum-colored uniform of the FBY. He had a little crystal dinner bell in each hand, and whenever he moved or made a gesture, the bells tinkled. The uniform itself was considerably the worse for wear.

He stood poised on the balls of his feet, looking at us with his shoulders hunched and his head forward. The skin of his face and scalp had a frosty, translucent brightness, like that of certain winter berries. He was completely bald.

"It's—is it Nipho?" Despoina asked doubtfully.

"I guess so," the man answered. He rubbed his nose, and the bell in his hand made a pretty noise. "Call me madam."

"What—how do you happen to be here?" she asked.

"They left me here when they closed the level off," Nipho told us. "They didn't want me with them any more. They tried to adjust me, you see. Yes, they tried to adjust me. But it didn't work."

"What do you mean by that?" I said.

He turned toward me. "Why, that they— Do you have the seeing? Look in my head."

I tried, and saw, after some effort, that the two hemispheres of his brain were crowded together by a rubbery fig-like structure on the left side. "Does it hurt?" I asked involuntarily.

"No, but there's always a fussing going on in my head. That's why I ring the bells. . . . They put it up my nose."

"You mean the FBY?" I asked.

He nodded, and there was a tiny tintinnabulation. "Yes, the FBY. I volunteered."

"What were they trying to do?" Despoina asked.

He turned a little to face her, and the bells tinkled again. "It's Despoina, isn't it? I can't see very well. Yes, Despoina. They were trying to make me like you."

"Like me? Why?" she asked.

"So I could do the things you do. It was an experiment. If it had worked, we would all have been adjusted to be like Despoina. We know what you people can do. We wanted to do it better and more easily."

I had noticed before an odd overlapping between us and our opponents. And Kyra had said that *they* had some of our techniques. But somehow it had never occurred to me that the FBY could be trying to duplicate our abilities for itself. I had thought their objective was simpler and more classic: to set up a new version of an old-style police state.

Ames had said his organization wasn't interested in Despoina. He ought to have known better. They were interested in whatever he was interested in. His organization keeps a tight grip on its men.

"It wasn't just the result of my work you wanted, then?" Despoina asked.

He pouted. "Oh—that too. Certainly that too. But Daddy-O used to say that what we needed was to take one of you people apart and find out what made him tick."

"Why are you two in such a sweat to get back to the surface? There's nothing up there that's so special. It's apt to be windy and damp."

Neither Despoina nor I had mentioned getting back to the surface; Nipho must be somewhat telephatic, I thought. It wasn't surprising, considering what had been done to him. The extra structure in his brain should have had some effect.

"Never mind why we want back," I told him. "Just take it that we do."

"Oh. But you could stay on down here with me, if you weren't so stubborn. It's not so bad, once one gets used to it. There's plenty to eat, and I sleep in the president's bed. It's lonely, though. I could use some company."

Despoina had been peering at him, her hands on her shoulders in one of the ritual attitudes. Now she said, "Do you know another way up, Nipho? A way that wasn't blocked off when they blew up G?"

"No, I don't," he answered readily. "There may be one, but I don't know about it. Why ask me, Spina? You know more about H than anybody else."

There it was again—the hint of familiarity between my lady and our pursuers. What had Ames been to her? Her lover? Probably. But I didn't like the idea at all.

Nipho turned to me. "I like you," he said. "I always wanted to be a girl. . . . Why don't you try to get up by the way you came down? That isn't blocked off."

I thought of the interminable descent, and the practical impossibility of getting up the shaft again, even with the pull of gravity much reduced. And at the top of the shaft was Ratty, eating desserts and unable to transmit a pile of planks without splintering it into excelsior. "We can't," I said. "It won't work."

"Oh. . . . Do you hear something?" He cocked his head in the manner of a dog picking up a scurry of mice.

I listened. "No," I said.

"Well, I do. I have good ears. It's"—he cocked his head again—"it's a digger. They're digging down to you. You could get up that way."

I still didn't hear anything. "A digger? Who's using it?" I said.

"Who do you suppose?" he asked, and launched himself at my throat.

The attack caught me by surprise. Usually, before a man jumps you, his eyes move, and this gives you a little warning. I went over backward, unable to break my fall, and hit my head on the rock floor. For a moment I lay stunned.

Nipho sat down on my chest and started to strangle me. I tried to throw him off, but all I could do was to thrash futilely with my legs in the air behind him. My upper arms were held down by his knees.

I got halfway up, and then he forced me down again. I made myself go limp, hoping he'd relax his hold, but it didn't work.

I was getting awfully short of air. My field of vision swam in a reddish haze. I was still trying to get my body up off the ground when Despoina, who had circled around back of Nipho, gave him a vicious rabbit punch on the nape of the neck.

Nipho grunted, a long, bubbling grunt, and collapsed sideways. I pushed him off me, got to my feet, and looked around for something to tie him up with.

I couldn't find anything. Despoina, seeing my difficulty, went into the little room with the American flag and came back with one of the president's bed sheets (no paper sheets for him). I managed to get it torn into long strips, and by the time Nipho came back to consciousness I had him tied up like a holiday turkey.

"How could you, dear?" he said, and then, more viciously, "You'll be sorry. Wait till Daddy-O gets through with you."

"I doubt it," I told him. I had to raise my voice to make myself heard. The corridor was full of a grinding, thudding noise that kept getting louder.

For a moment I couldn't think what it was. Despoina put her lips close to my ear. "It's the digger," she said.

23

THE NOSE of the digger broke through the rock roof in a flood of diamond light. It was like the misty aureole of rainbow color one sees at the bottom of a high waterfall, and for a moment I thought of ferny grottoes and cool greenery. Then the big helical stairway slid silently through the fifteen-foot-wide opening and made a noiseless contact with the rock floor.

Two men in the familiar plum-colored uniform were standing on the lower steps. One of them reached behind him and touched a lever on the central shaft around which the helix was mounted. The digging cone retracted, the noise ceased. There was an effect of seafaring about it, as if men at the prow of a ship had put her in to shore and run her up on the beach.

I saw other men on the steps above them. The abrupt cessation of the noise of the digger made me feel confused, and this feeling was increased when the two men stepped lightly from the lower turn of the coil and came toward the president's office, their hands on their side arms.

They had certainly seen us. I did not know what to do. For a moment I felt utterly lost, as if an invisible thread I had been following had broken without warning and left me empty-handed in the midst of unknown dangers. The rock walls and corridors around me had a pointless artificiality, like the setting for an insipid play. Then Despoina put her hand on my shoulder, and my mind steadied.

I was of the Wicca, after all, and though the men who had dug down through G to capture us would certainly be on their guard against any of our devices, I might be able to do something. Kyra had taught me a good many things.

The FBY men were still a few yards away. "Come along, you two," the man in the lead said in a brisk voice. "We're taking you topside."

"No, you're not," I answered. I pushed Despoina behind me for her better protection. "I want to speak to the chief."

"What!" The man in the lead (he was blond and clean-cut, very much a member of an elite) gave a hard, snorting laugh. "Nonsense! Prisoners don't ask to speak to the chief. Come along."

"We're not prisoners," I replied. I unbuttoned my right breast pocket and pulled out the glass bottle labeled "Tums."

"In this bottle," I told the two men, "are spores of a new form of plague. It is a mutated form of the yeast that causes neurolytic plague, but it is even deadlier. If I undo the cap on the bottle and pull out the cotton, you and everybody on that digging contraption will be dead in less than sixty seconds. The lady and I, because of our physical peculiarities, are immune."

His jaw set. "And if I simply stun you?"

"There's a good chance the bottle will break as I fall."

He gave me a piercing look. Plainly, he thought I might be lying, but he couldn't be sure. For a long moment we stood facing each other, locked in a mutual immobility. Then, without turning his head, he said to the man with him, "Davis, please go tell our head that the prisoner would like to speak with him. Tell him the circumstances."

"Very well, captain." Davis went toward the digger at a brisk walk, leaving his superior and me once more staring into each other's eyes.

I kept my gaze steady, but my mind was elsewhere. I was running over the small armory of devices Kyra had taught me, wondering which of them would serve. Fith-fath? Almost certainly not—we couldn't keep it up long enough, and even if we were able to evade the FBY men's eyes, we wouldn't be able to get past them on the helical stair. They would detect us by touch, if not by sight.

Wasn't there anything else? "Magic" indubitably works; but its processes, generally speaking, have an organic slowness like the growth of a flower. It is difficult to hurry them. I remembered something

Kyra had told me once, while she tossed up the athame and caught it again: that the dead have set up a pattern that can sometimes be contacted and used. That is why they are called "the mighty dead."

While these thoughts ran through my mind, the FBY man and I had stood confronting each other, our eyes locked. Now from the helical stair behind him a man stepped to the floor and came toward us at an even pace.

He was older than the others, his hair lightly gray, and his bearing had the ease of uncontested authority. When he got to me he looked me up and down for an instant and then said, "What do you want?" in a civil, but quite impersonal way.

"We want to go back to the surface," I told him, "but not under guard, and not as prisoners. You are to let us go completely free."

As I spoke, I became aware that my mind had separated into at least three parts: the part with which I was speaking to Daddy-O; the part which was anxiously trying to contact one of the patterns of power; and the part which was planning an over-all strategy. Yet "I" was in command of all three, and I felt as easy about it as a man might who was simultaneously smoking a pipe and reading a book. Despoina was standing close behind me, her hand on my shoulder, and that may have had something to do with it. There never was a greater witch than my lady.

Daddy-O laughed. He sounded genuinely amused. "This is nonsense," he observed, more to the other FBY man than to me or Despoina. "Sewell—that's his name, I believe—Sewell is bluffing. If he can do what he says, why doesn't he simply do it? I doubt he would be restrained by any considerable scruple for life. Handcuff him, Phillips, or throw a net over him. Perhaps a net would be best. But bring him along. I want to examine him." He turned to go.

I drew a deep breath. I had failed—no, I hadn't. Something was putting me on, as I might put on clothing, something old and powerful; a heart that was not my own was beating, steady and strong, within my breast. Now I knew what to do.

I knew the meaning of the double axe.

"Wait!" I said.

I must have put considerable authority into the syllable, for Daddy-O turned half around to look at me. "Well?" he said.

I gave him look for look. I could feel him trying to probe my mind; but then, he had three minds to probe. He wasn't getting anywhere with it.

"I haven't much scruple for your life," I told him, "but we could be useful to each other. Don't you know that?"

This time he didn't laugh. "How?" he said.

"You have the organization; *we* have the power," I said. "You'll never find out unless we choose to tell you. Our people can be silent. The inquisitors used to complain that we slept on the rack.

"Force won't do it. But a free agreement might. A *modus vivendi*—we can work out the details later—would be of great mutual benefit."

Daddy-O was, I am sure, an intelligent man. In some respects, he had a better mind than I. But it had one serious limitation: he couldn't imagine anyone genuinely actuated by motives very different from his own.

He knew we Wicca have "supernormal" abilities. He coveted them for the sake of personal and organizational aggrandizement. He saw life in terms of power; it didn't occur to him that we would no more surrender our "secrets" to him than we would have surrendered them to the inquisition. He thought the craft was a bag of valuable tricks, whereas it is a glowing faith.

He hesitated, chewing on his lower lip. I could see that his pride of caste was warring with the plausibility of my argument (and, despite some obvious holes, it *was* superficially plausible). He was just on the point of telling Phillips to turn us loose for the time being, when Nipho, who had been lying unnoticed on the spot on the rock floor where I had left him tied, piped up.

"Take him to pieces, Daddy-O!" he yelled. "Take him to pieces and find what makes him tick!"

That tore it. The big chief's face set hard. Nipho's unceremonious interruption had recalled him to himself—or, more accurately, to his former conviction that the Wicca "powers" were nothing but a matter of physiology.

In a moment he was going to tell Phillips to throw a net over us and prod us up the stair. I hadn't any time at all. I made the bull-leap.

Now, there has been a lot of nonsense talked about Crete. In particular, the general public has accepted, for almost three-quarters of a century, things as genuinely Cretan that never existed except in the mind of the excavators. "Creativity" is something to be avoided in restoring long-buried works of art. Insight helps, and patience. But if an archaeologist wants to be "creative," he would do better to take up knots and fancy ropework.

Not all the bull-leaping frescoes and statuettes fall into this category. Two or three have, in fact, been correctly restored. The sport did exist. But the real importance of bull-leaping is as a physical symbol for a psychological thing.

Over the horns, then, and through the air. Dizzy and glad, a little rapture-sick. Dizzy and glad, through the air, and straight at Daddy-O's head.

He did not want to receive me. But he had had no warning, and I—or the third of my mind that was doing the leaping—was augmented by that other, long-breathless force. Time is different there, you see. But it had been a long time, four millennia at least, since the man who had set up that pattern had seen the blessed light of the sun.

Now came a very odd thing. I had ousted Daddy-O from his cranium; I could feel him raging impotently around me. But "I" still remained in command of Sam Sewell's body; I saw through his eyes, drew his breath. I had a divided consciousness, that is all. It would be a waste of words to try to describe it further.

I raised the chief's hand to his lips and had him rub his lower face. "Ah—Nipho, be quiet," I made him say. And then, to Phillips, "Stun him, if he keeps talking."

He turned—I made him turn—toward Sam Sewell. "Very well, you may go," I said through boss-man's lips. "You are to report to our headquarters at your earliest convenience. Any considerable delay will result in trouble. You understand? You will be kept under surveillance."

Sam Sewell nodded. "Yes, I understand."

"Very well, then. Go." (I hoped I wasn't repeating myself too much.) I had him turn away from me.

Sam Sewell walked past him, Despoina following. Her hand was still on Sewell's arm. Together they started up the helical stair.

Sam Sewell felt drained and weak. But that could be excused, and the FBY men made way for them. For the moment—as long as I could control the chief's body—they were safe.

And now the last of the odd things of that odd time happened. (How many parts does the mind have? Now I had four.) Odd, but simple: I knew who I was.

I would think about it more later, when I had time. But I knew who I was.

24

THEY HAD made way for us, we had started up the helical stair. But they were only a few feet behind us. As they moved up after us I could hear the faint clank and jangle of the gadgets and grenades they wore at their belts. We did not dare go as fast as we could.

We climbed. Around and around, tracing out the big circle with the twelve-foot diameter that the digger had made. We would stop for a moment or two, catch our breath, and then go on again. We climbed.

Daddy-O, behind us, was not doing very well. Sam Sewell's occupation of him was turning out to be deleterious. His heart beat was weak and irregular, his skin was dry and flushed, his field of vision blurred. Now and again I had him stop to lean on the arms of his lieutenants, and twice I had him reply, to their solicitious questions, "Nonsense! I'm quite all right. Just a little tired."

This was wildly untrue. Daddy-O, boiling with rage outside his cranium, knew it. I am uncertain what the reason was for his physical distress; Kyra, when we discussed it later, said that the autonomic nervous system's action was inhibited by my usurpation of Daddy-O's body. When I protested that the autonomic nervous system keeps on functioning even in deep unconsciousness, she replied that personality persists even when there is no awareness of it. I suppose a non-technical explanation would be that it doesn't do a body any good to be run from the outside.

The big chief's frequent stops to rest had widened the gap between us and his men. We could climb a little faster now, and we did. Around and around, around and around, we climbed.

But now I was confronted by a cruel dilemma. I had no particular reason to feel concern for the FBY's chief, but I wasn't a murderer. If I didn't let him back inside his own body fairly soon, I'd have his death on my hands. More cogently, if he collapsed, I'd have a new FBY chief to deal with, and I didn't think I could manage the bull-leap twice. But if I let Daddy-O run himself again, his first act would be to order Despoina and me arrested. And the next thing would be "taking us apart to find out what made us tick."

I compromised. I moved out just a little, enough to let him put a few tendrils of his own inside and start his heart to working properly. But my action was a tiny bit too late. I had misjudged the time.

Too late. The smooth nervous impulses of normal heart beat had gone into a wild jangle of conflicting innervation. Daddy-O, back in his body too late, gave a bubbling moan and fell down on the stair.

His men gathered anxiously around him. I had withdrawn my control of him the instant he fell. Now Despoina and I, wasting no words on external communication, began to run for all we were worth.

No shout came from behind us. I suppose they were too occupied with their attentions to their collapsed leader to notice the extent to which Despoina and I had speeded up. The babble of their worried voices receded, and the tingling sensation between my shoulder blades—the expectation of a bullet, a bolt from a stun gun, or a tear-gas grenade—began to die away. By the time exhaustion forced Despoina and me to a more moderate pace, I had begun to hope that our flight would escape notice.

We had come up a long, long way. There were only a few inches between the edges of the stair treads and the sides of the shaft, and I could not see the bottom. But even the partial glances I caught made me dizzy. The pressure in my ears kept changing. Up through H, clean through G, buried in its rubble; and now we must, I thought, be nearly done with F. I could see an enlarging round spot of light at the top of the shaft. Yes, we had come up a long way.

We were nearly at the top. Still no shouts from behind us, no noise of pursuit. I had time to marvel at the size of the digger and wonder how the FBY had ever got it into place. The logistical difficulties of getting a thing that size into F and started digging must have been enormous. . . . Closer and closer; only a few feet now. Then I saw, with a staggering shock of dismay, that two guards had been posted at the top of the shaft.

Despoina saw them at the same moment as I; her fingers tightened on my arm. But if Sam Sewell was dismayed into a momentary helplessness, the pattern Sam had contacted half an hour ago was not.

He pushed his way up through me as a swimmer pushes his way through water. I felt my face—Sam Sewell's ordinary, plastic face, molded by long-dead plastic-shaping fingers. It was not painful in a physical sense, but it took great resolution for me not to resist it. If he had put me on earlier as I might put on a suit of clothing, he was now rearranging his garment.

He and I were willing ourselves together. The boundaries of our two natures were growing blurred. A strength and wisdom not my own lay at my disposal. It was a heady, self-intoxicated experience—and yet, one to inspire a deep humility.

Despoina and I had reached the top of the shaft. The guards were looking at us uncertainly. I pushed Despoina in front of me unceremoniously, as a prisoner might be pushed. To the guards I said, "The chief's had a heart attack. Go get a doctor, and a stretcher with straps. Hurry, now."

The voice I had spoken in was not my own. It was lower in pitch, with more force in the plosives and a longer lingering on the sibilants. It was, in fact, Phillips' voice.

"Yes, sir," said one of the guards. "Excuse me, sir, I didn't recognize you at first." He hesitated. "The girl, sir—"

"She's a prisoner," I answered, frowning. (How odd my face felt, with the muscles and their points of attachment in the wrong places!) "I told you two to hurry. This is an emergency."

"Yes, sir." The guards turned and made off at a running lope.

Despoina and I took the last two steps out of the shaft. We were on F, in a part of that extensive level that was not very familiar to me. I thought the closest access to E lay to the right. But that was the way the guards were going. It would be better to take another path.

We took the corridor to the left, then, as rapidly as we could. That was not very fast, for we were both exhausted, and Despoina, particularly, was almost on the edge of collapse.

The "pattern of power" that had been a man once, millennia ago, was leaving me. Gently and quietly, a little at a time, it was withdrawing from me, disentangling itself from my body, my mind. I felt a little sad. But it was good to be only myself again.

We had gone only a few feet further when Despoina had to stop and lean against the wall to rest. My heart smote me when I saw how pale she was. But I did not dare let her rest for more than a minute or two.

"I know," she gasped when I said we must move on. "They've left the shaft . . . and . . . we didn't come all this way . . . to be caught."

Seconds later we heard the sound of explosions at the end of the corridor from which we had come. They were followed by a shudder, a tremble, through the very fabric of the rock.

What was happening? Were our pursuers trying to blow up the whole level in order to rid themselves of us? Surely not; they must be lobbing grenades into the cross-corridors at random, trying to flush us out.

But the ominous shudder through the rock had given me an idea; perhaps it was the last legacy of the pattern that had been a man once in Crete, millennia ago. I knew where I had seen Jaeger.

"Hurry, hurry!" I said to Despoina. "We've got to get to the lower gallery!"

25

WE HAD taken cover behind an outcropping of rock to the left of, and a few hundred feet distant from, the entrance to the lower gallery. I thought the rock would keep our pursuers from picking us up with snooper-scopes. And I believed (I had a dim recollection of Jaeger's testifying to this effect before a senate investigating committee) that the rock ceiling was particularly strong at this point. Strong enough? That was something we'd have to find out.

There was another good reason for selecting this spot as a redoubt. Despoina had told me, as we hurried along, that any sound made here would be picked up, amplified, and reechoed from about the middle of the gallery. Unless the men pursuing us were more familiar with the acoustic properties of the gallery than I thought they were, they would probably think we were hiding somewhere inside if.

We waited. It was part of my plan to use the tidal stresses the moving moon makes through the solid rocks of her primary. Magic would not help us much now, except to supply the illusion that I hoped would trick our opponents into action. I would try to accomplish a physical effect by physical means.

I used the sight and saw, through hundreds and hundreds of feet of construction and rock, that the reddish circle of the moon was mounting steadily in the sky. The ideal time to put my plan into action would be when she was a little past the meridian.

Our pursuers were going to a lot of trouble to capture us. I could hear their voices as they gave orders over walkie-talkies to their men on the levels above us, and they were bringing up searchlights and racks of small shells. The light was poor, but they were visible enough. All these men, to catch two unarmed Wicca! It had its amusing side. I wondered fleetingly why they didn't simply rush us. But they didn't know exactly where we were, and they couldn't be quite sure we weren't, after all, carrying the spores of some new and deadlier form of plague.

I speculated about the racks of shells. Hand grenades? Almost certainly not—they had those at their belts, and would be reluctant to use them on us, in any case. They wanted us intact, and they wanted what we were carrying intact. The shells probably held tear gas or some anesthetic. It would take a good deal of provocation to make the FBY throw grenades directly at where they thought we were. The grenade-throwing on F had been intended solely to scare us out.

There was a rumble, and then an amplified voice, loud and toneless, addressed us. "Come out, and you will not be hurt," it said. "We will respect the agreement Commissioner Harris made with you. We promise you immunity. Come out, and you will not be hurt. Come out, and you will not be hurt."

It was a promise; I felt a prickle of temptation. We Wicca are trained in scruple for life, if we do not possess it to begin with. Perhaps we could arrange a *modus vivendi* after all.

I put my lips against Despoina's ear and said, very softly, "Can you pick up their thoughts?"

She shook her head. "No," she answered in the same cautious manner. "They're shielding."

That in itself was suspicious—why should they be shielding, if they were sincere in their offer?—but it wasn't conclusive.

I reflected. Then I pried a few pebbles loose from the surface of the rock and pocked them—one, two, three, four—against the adjacent rock wall. In a second or two a noise, almost exactly like the noise of a stun gun at full charge, came echoing out of the middle of the lower gallery.

There was an immediate burst of activity—order-issuing, saluting, and jumping about with matériel—from our antagonists. The amplified voice stopped in mid-phrase. In the confusion somebody let his mental shield drop briefly, and I, who am no more than a fair telepath, caught the words, ". . . bastards. When we catch them, I'll take pleasure in dissecting out the girl's nervous system personally."

Well, that was conclusive enough. I sighed softly. Now that we had nothing but my plan to fall back on, I realized how rickety it was.

What would they do next? The moon was almost on the meridian. I remembered that Jaeger, a geologist testifying against the construction of the levels system, had said that the whole site was geologically unsound, but that the lower gallery was so weak the work of trying to reinforce it would bring its roof tumbling in. The legislators had heeded him enough to omit the gallery from the scheme of construction. It was more of an effect than witnesses before committees usually have.

Our antagonists were loading up their belts with shells from the rack. Whatever they were going to do, it was time for Despoina and me to begin our work.

When I had asked her, just before our pursuers had come up with us, whether it would be possible for us to make the phantasm of a man, she had pinched her lip and replied that it would be difficult. Such projection needed a calm, clear mind. But when I had explained what I was aiming at, she had agreed to try. Now, on our knees facing each other, between the outcropping of rock and the rock wall, we began the simple rite.

The most difficult thing, as she had foretold, was keeping our minds on the work. If it had not been for Kyra's training, I could never have done it. Curiosity about the noises our enemies were making kept breaking in. But at least we were finished. On the rock floor between us a whitish ropey thing lay, twitching weakly with life from our life.

It could take care of itself for an instant. I risked a glance out, and saw that the FBY men were moving slowly into the gallery. Two big searchlights, behind them, warred with the place's shadows.

As the men advanced, they made sowing motions with their hands and I heard a series of faint plops. What—? Oh, they were wearing gas masks.

I waited until they were all within the gallery. Their movements were cautious; they were looking for us in every shadow and behind every stalactite. I smelled a sweetish smell, and knew they were using anesthetizing gas.

Now. The moon was just past the meridian; it was time. I motioned to Despoina. We made the phantasm stand up.

It was just under six feet tall, faintly luminous, and as unsubstantial as a ghost. In fact, strictly speaking, it *was* a ghost, being made of what old-fashioned mediums called ectoplasm. But I thought it would pass muster, if only I could startle our enemies enough.

The phantasm floated forward, until it stood just within the mouth of the gallery. As loudly as I could, I bellowed, "You sons of bitches, now you're in our trap!"

They must have heard my shout as coming from all sides at once. They spun round, hands on their guns, ready to fire. And they saw the phantom, its arm raised over its shoulder, poised to throw a bomb at them.

Some nervous character fired at it; I heard the coughing roar of a mini-burp. My ruse was going to work; it was working. In the next minute everybody would have been throwing grenades. But Despoina, who had been supplying most of the plasm for the phantasm, gave a little moan and fell forward. She had fainted. And the phantasm collapsed like an umbrella shutting up.

There was a crisscrossing of shouts within the gallery. An authoritative voice overrode them. "Silence! That was nothing but a trick, one of their magic tricks. They are unarmed. Arnaudi and Bacon, stand guard at the entrance. The rest of you, go on with your search!"

Their famous discipline held. Arnaudi and Bacon detached themselves from the group, and the others went on with their cautious investigation of the lower gallery.

I felt sick with defeat. In a minute or two they would realize we weren't in the gallery, and start looking elsewhere for us. What were we to do? If we left the shelter of the rock outcrop, Arnaudi and Bacon would see us; and if, by some miracle, we got past them to one of the exits from D, the FBY would have men stationed at the top.

What could we do? We might be able to evade them for a few hours, perhaps even for a couple of days. They were sure to get us in the end. And then . . .

Would they really dissect—? Of course they would. They had blown up a whole level, with half a thousand people in it, merely to insure that we Wicca should no longer be able to get to H. They certainly would not balk at a little dissection. And then Despoina and I would have the opportunity—the very undesirable opportunity—of finding out just what the FBY man had meant, that night on the edge of the burial ground, when he said, "If they can be turned . . ."

Despoina stirred against the rough rock where she was lying, and opened her eyes. In a thread of a voice, she said, "The rock."

For a moment I hated her. What did she mean by that? If she had not fainted, we would not now be in this desperate pass. Then I looked at the inner side of the rock and saw, about shoulder level, a half-detached, roughly globular rock chunk about the size of a baseball.

In a moment I was prying at it frantically. If I could get it loose—if it could be thrown—Why not? It was worth trying. We couldn't be any worse off.

I got the chunk loose just as, to judge from their footsteps, the FBY finished searching the gallery and started back toward the entrance. The moon was well past her peak. With only an instant to aim, I threw the globe, baseball-pitcher fashion, for all I was worth.

I had aimed at a point near the entrance, at a cluster of stalactites depending from the gallery's low roof. I missed the first; my rock crashed into the second stalactite. There was a dull, hollow noise, and then the whole lower half of the limestone mass broke off. It struck the gallery floor only a few feet from the advancing FBY.

Even then it might not have worked. But the men on guard at the entrance had seen the flight of my missile and heard its impact. One of them panicked. He threw a hand grenade at us.

It did no harm. But somebody inside the gallery, hearing the crashing rock and then the explosion, decided it was an attack. He threw a grenade toward the middle of the gallery. He must have heard the explosion of Arnaudi's grenade as coming from there.

The beams of the searchlights danced about crazily. Someone threw another grenade, and then another. In the next half-minute there must have been a dozen explosions, interspersed with rifle fire and the coughs of a mini-burp.

The authoritative voice was bawling desperately, trying to reestablish order. But by then it was already too late. I felt a long, grinding shudder through the floor.

The roof of the gallery began to shake. It bulged downward, lower and lower, like a straining membrane. Then it broke, and ton upon ton of earth and rock came pouring in.

I had gathered Despoina in my arms and stood pressed tight against the rock face, praying the rock here would hold. A man—Arnaudi or Bacon—ran toward us, yelling something. A section of the roof fell behind him. Then a shower of earth covered him up. The noise of pouring rock grew louder, and then slowly grew less, and ceased.

It seemed to be over. The lower gallery had collapsed completely; all sound of voices from within it had died. But I had felt another warning tremor from below. I stood waiting, holding Despoina so tightly my arms ached.

There was a long, enormous roar, that somehow sounded melancholy. Another, another, and the roaring grew nearer. The floor tipped under me. I clutched at the rock.

The floor sloped even more violently. Off to the right, where the main-level structure was, I heard an advancing noise, a mighty, dreadful roaring. I knew what it was. No need to speculate—the levels were falling in.

Everything before me was abruptly wiped out in a cascade of falling rock. There was nothing to breathe; the air seemed solid. Too dazed to be frightened, I held Despoina in my arms and waited for life or death.

I had braced my feet against the rock outcropping. Now it, too, broke away. I felt myself slipping forward helplessly.

More rock. A barrier that I clutched at the last moment. And then, from the riven levels hundreds of feet above us, the glorious light of the moon broke in.

I sighed shakily. Despoina stirred in my arms, and I set her down carefully on the sloping floor. The air was full of a choking dust. It settled heavily for a long time.

26

THE MOON was our guide. Looking up I could see, between the jagged side of the shaft and the edge of the gigantic rubble heap, clear spaces through which it might be possible to climb. I leaned out from the shallow, slowly sinking ledge, and caught at the end of a length of construction steel over my head. It gave a little, but it was solidly weighted under tons of rubble. I was able to pull myself up on it and straddle it.

From there I leaned over for Despoina and gave her my hand. When we were both astride the girder, we inched our way along it briefly, took a couple of steps on the sliding rubble, and caught at the skeleton of a steel door that stuck out higher up, from where D had been. From here we were able to grasp a reinforced concrete column that must have been a roof support. Our progress was painfully slow, partly because we had to test everything before we put our weight on it, and partly because we were desperately tired.

We worked our way up past the protruding legs of office furniture, crumpled refrigerators, sections of steel bookcases, broken lavatory basins, fifty-gallon drums of coolants, shattered power equipment, steel bedsteads—all the material side of an autarkic private world. And now that world had sunk into the depths.

When we got to where level C had been, we had a bit of luck. At the very edge of the excavated level an escalator was still standing. It was not running, of course, and it hung out over nothing, but we could climb it at our own pace.

After some thirty feet there was a landing, and the escalator made a turn of 180 degrees. We went on climbing. At the next landing there was an interruption. A concrete boulder lay between us and the next steps.

It could be climbed over, I thought, but we were so tired that we had to have rest. The escalator seemed solid enough. I had seen a foam rubber mattress hanging limply out of the rubble near us. Telling Despoina to wait, I snagged the mattress with a length of angle iron, and drew it up to the landing.

I spread it out on the hard floor. Then we lay down, and with Despoina in my arms I fell into the deepest and most refreshing sleep that ever I had in my life.

When I woke, the moon was halfway down the sky. Despoina opened her eyes and smiled at me. They say you can't tell colors by moonlight; that's nonsense. Her hair was still a burning red.

Without a word being spoken, we began to make love. What surprised me most was how easy everything was. But then, this pleasure had been in preparation for a long while.

When I had first met Despoina she had been the great witch, the high priestess, naked to the waist, but clothed in authority. Next she had been my companion, a woman by my side in stresses and dangers. Now it was neither of these that I embraced, but the very spirit, wild and sweet, of the ageless, immortal earth.

When we were satisfied, we slept for a little while. Then—reluctantly, but the moon was getting low—we left our bed and pulled on our clothes.

We got around the concrete mass without much difficulty. At the top of the escalator the floor had broken away, but a service ladder, seemingly quite strong, was still against the rock and led up toward level A.

When the ladder ended, I reached out for a pipe. This came away when I put weight on it; I looked about for something else, and found, above and to the right, a large square opening.

From what I remembered of A's geography, this would lead to one of the many subsidiary entrances. There would be a passage, sloping gradually upward, and then we would be on the surface again.

The trouble was in getting up to the opening. Despoina, below me, saw what the difficulty was. She called up, "There's the back of an office chair where I can reach it. If you wedge the end under the top ladder rung, you can climb up the slats."

"Okay," I answered; "hand it up."

The chairback was sturdy oak, the kind of chair one finds in seminar rooms. I turned the concave face toward the wall, hooked the top under the rung, and went up the slats before I had time to worry about falling back. I threw the upper part of my body forward into the opening. At the cost of two barked shins, I was inside. Then I reached down for Despoina. She was bigger than Kyra, but she didn't weigh very much more.

The passage was lighted by a fluorescent glow, dimmer than the light of the dying moon outside. There was a draft of air down it from the still distant and invisible surface.

I said, "Despoina, how did you happen to know Ames?"

She laughed. "Has that been on your mind all this time?"

"Yes. You did know him, you know."

"I never denied it." She sighed.

"When I first began to dream about you," she went on, "I never could see your face. . . . Do you know now who you are, Sam?"

"I think so. I'm the devil."

"You're the person our persecutors called the devil," she amended. "They gave that name to the male counterpart of the high priestess, the other focus of power in the circle. You're of the old blood, Sam."

"I know. I mean, now I know."

"Yes. . . . When I first began to have dreams about you, I never could see your face. I had to hunt for you, and the most likely place to find you seemed in the FBY, who obviously were in possession of some of our techniques."

"So Ames—"

"Ames was one of the people I thought might be you. He passed the first tests well, but failed further along.

"Ames's contacts with me attracted the attention of his superiors, and Gerald was assigned to spy on us."

"Who was Gerald?" I asked.

"He was the man you saw die of the pulmonary form of the plague on level F1. Don't you remember, when Kyra first saw you she said, 'You're not Gerald'? She didn't know he was dead.

"I had been inclined to take him at face value, but the elders distrusted him. They set a trap for him, a trap an innocent man would have ignored. His death was the proof of his guilt. But we didn't mean him to die."

We had been walking along, slowly but steadily, while we talked. Now I said, "Was Nipho another of your candidates?"

She laughed. "No. He saw me with Ames a few times, and remembered me."

I sighed. "Are you still vexed?" she asked.

"Vexed? Yes, I suppose I am. I'm wondering what the future will be like—

"After the plagues, society fell apart because people could no longer cooperate. But what I'm carrying in my pockets—what we went down to level H to get—will change that. And then what will happen, Dess? If people can cooperate again, won't they cooperate for mutual destruction? That is what has always happened in the past."

She nodded. "Yes, there is a chance. But the plagues have produced physical changes in people, and not all of them are reversible. We are different from what we used to be. If there is the possibility of the old bad world again, there is also the possibility of building it up better than it was. The risk is worth taking. We have come through so much! We must be hopeful about this."

We had reached the very end of the passage. The night lay before us. The moon had set. The sky was quite dark. Cassiopeia was at its highest point above Polaris, and the bright stars of Orion burned in the east.

"Which is it, Despoina," I asked musingly, "'the clockwork of the heavens, impressive in a rather boring Newtonian way,' or 'the army of unalterable law'?"

"You are well-read, Sam," she answered. Her profile glinted faintly in the starlight. "I don't know the answer. But perhaps it is enough that we have left the underworld forever, and can say with a mightier poet, 'We issued forth, and saw again the stars.'"